I was two steps de
I looked up and sa
recognize me and
aid.

He was inches away from me when I fell into his arms and began crying. All the anger I'd felt toward him, the hurt he caused me, the stupid ways he'd played me...they all meant nothing in this moment. He was here when I needed him the most. And I could no longer hold my tears back as he stood without a word and let me soak his shirt with sobs for minutes, only occasionally stroking my hair to bring me comfort.

"Maybe we should go for a walk," he finally said.

"A walk sounds good."

Dear Reader,

There is a special connection that women have with the beautiful items found in their homes. For some, it's with their favorite jeans, the purses delicately hanging in closets or the jewelry or books they've acquired over time. For me, it's always been with my shoes. To this day, I can recall moments while wearing each one.

So, I knew if I was going to tell the story of a young woman moving beyond her list of "shoulds"—many of us know these well: should get a degree, should have a successful career and be married by X age, should be a certain weight with an envious waist-to-hip ratio, etc.—I *had* to feature the shoes that symbolized her journey.

Enter *The Shoe Diaries*: the fun, vulnerable, sometimes painful, but ultimately, hopeful story of Reagan Doucet. Like many of us, she spent her twenties building a perfect life until she realized she was like the hot-pink stilettos that went unworn in her closet for years— beautiful to look at, but unfulfilled. When she takes on a "risk list," Reagan learns to trust herself again and finds love with an unexpected person.

This book begins my Friendship Chronicles series for Harlequin Special Edition. I can't wait for you to meet these dynamic women. In different ways, each of their stories speak to the angst we all have around succeeding in our careers, our desires for love and the beauty in the friend connections we make.

I hope you enjoy!

Darby Baham

The Shoe Diaries

DARBY BAHAM

HARLEQUIN

SPECIAL
EDITION

HARLEQUIN®

SPECIAL EDITION™

Recycling programs for this product may not exist in your area.

ISBN-13: 978-1-335-40836-5

The Shoe Diaries

Copyright © 2022 by Darby Baham

All rights reserved. No part of this book may be used or reproduced in any manner whatsoever without written permission except in the case of brief quotations embodied in critical articles and reviews.

This is a work of fiction. Names, characters, places and incidents are either the product of the author's imagination or are used fictitiously. Any resemblance to actual persons, living or dead, businesses, companies, events or locales is entirely coincidental.

This edition published by arrangement with Harlequin Books S.A.

For questions and comments about the quality of this book, please contact us at CustomerService@Harlequin.com.

Harlequin Enterprises ULC
22 Adelaide St. West, 41st Floor
Toronto, Ontario M5H 4E3, Canada
www.Harlequin.com

Printed in U.S.A.

Darby Baham (she/her) is a debut author with Harlequin Special Edition and a New Yorker of five years who sometimes desperately misses the sprawling shoe closet she had while living in Maryland. She's had personal blog posts appear in the *Washington Post*'s relationship vertical and worked in the communications industry for more than two decades. The New Orleans native is also a lover of big laughs and books that swallow you into their world.

Books by Darby Baham

Harlequin Special Edition

The Friendship Chronicles

The Shoe Diaries

Visit the Author Profile page
at Harlequin.com for more titles.

To all the little Black girls, like me,
who devoured the rare romance stories they
read about women who looked like them.
I hope you know that love for you isn't rare at all.
It's actually quite beautiful in its commonness.

Part 1: Life is a Journey Made Better with Great Shoes

"A journey of a thousand miles begins with a single step (and a great pair of shoes!)."
—paraphrased from Lao-tzu

Prologue

February 13, 2016

"With this ring, I thee wed, and with it, I bestow upon thee the treasures of my mind, heart and hands…"

Staring at my friends from my seat, I noticed more than just their words as they recited their vows. I saw their hands clasped together throughout the ceremony, and the smiles they wore even through their tears; the way they focused on each other like no one else was present even while a hundred and fifty of us stared at them with glee. But most important, I saw the love that was undeniable between the two of them. Strange, but I was all at once happy and sad, amazed and hurt. In them I saw hope for a future. Here were two people who'd found love and decided that nothing else was more important than their union. Yet, standing less than two feet away from them, I also saw the man I'd hoped would be my future—and it hurt me to my core to know that we would never have this same moment.

Every few minutes I caught myself peeking over at him during the ceremony, hoping he would turn to me, and we would have some kind of knowing thought between us. That we would have a brief second where no words were necessary, and through our eyes, we'd say, "I know it didn't work for us, but I still love you." I craved that moment more than anything I'd ever wanted before, wishing with all my might he would just look over. Just glance at me… and smile.

That look never happened.

I knew from the moment my friends announced their engagement that their wedding would be special. They were *those* kinds of people. The ones who managed to turn something very simple into the most extraordinary event you would attend, so it was pretty much a guarantee that their wedding was going to be *a show*. And Candice and Lance did not disappoint. Their ceremony, cocktail hour and reception were all held at the famed Loews Philadelphia Hotel—platinum-style decor and black-tie attire requested. I just hoped I could get past my feelings of seeing my ex-boyfriend, Jake, on the big day, and that I could experience the love all around me without disappointment in my heart.

For months I'd known he was going to be there. Well, that wasn't true. For months I'd known he was going to be in the wedding party, which is an entirely different thing to handle. And yet, I'd managed not to make a big deal about it. I attended the engagement party with no problems. I broke bread with his sister at the bridal shower like nothing was wrong. I shopped for my dress for the wedding, packed the last few days before the wedding, made my way to Philly, spent time with friends the night before and still hadn't quite let myself think about the fact that I would see the man I'd wanted to marry stand up in support of our friends who were planning to spend the rest of their lives together.

That was until I stepped off the elevator and into the lobby of the floor where the ceremony was being held. Then suddenly, I felt my heart thud in my chest and my feet go numb. *What am I doing?* I questioned. How was I going to make it through tonight?

I was two seconds away from having a complete meltdown—hyperventilating, ugly tears, the whole nine—when I peered down at my shoes, and they somehow helped me will myself into gaining control of my emotions. I took one slow, deep breath, then another, eyed my friends who'd joined me that weekend to see if they noticed my momentary freak-out, and quietly composed myself before taking another step forward. Thankfully, Robin and Jennifer were far too busy scoping out the crowd to notice my meltdown, but they eventually realized I was no longer in step with them and turned around to see me stuck in place next to the elevator. I was nearly twenty steps behind them by then.

"Are you all right?" mouthed Jennifer, concern on her face.

I nodded, then changed my mind and shook my head, then after one more breath, nodded again.

As I began walking toward them, I focused my mind on my girls, who were impeccably dressed, smiles ablaze with anticipation for the evening, and reminded myself of one important thing: this night was not about me. I refused to let them know all the thoughts running through my head, and I refused to be that person who takes over someone else's moment with their drama.

Instead, I straightened out my floor-length, sky blue gown, swept the bottom of the dress to my left side and gathered it in my hand while the three of us walked into the ceremony hall. Confidently. Our curves swaying with power. My crystal-sequined shoes glistening underneath and helping to center my five-foot-three frame as we made our way to our seats.

"Reagan, you sure you're all right?" Robin whispered in my ear as we sat down.

"I'm sure."

"Because, I mean, we would all understand if you weren't."

"No, seriously, I'm fine. Just had a moment, but everything is good now."

"Okay," she replied with just a slight twinge of disbelief and a quick tap of her hand on my thigh.

We'd barely had time to settle in our seats when a hush came over the crowd as the pastor and Lance walked to the front of the room. Lance was beaming. His outfit was sharp—crisp black bow tie, suit tailored to perfection, cuff links just slightly peeking out—but the real standout was the smile he couldn't get rid of throughout his entire walk up to the front. Once the men arrived at their positions, the music started up, and two by two, each bridesmaid entered the aisle with a groomsman on her arm. They walked slowly but with purpose, their eyes focused solely on their destination.

When it was Jake's turn, my heart skipped a beat as soon as he entered the room. I watched him as he offered his arm for his bridesmaid to hold and walked her down the long, silver-carpeted aisle. I yearned for him as his lips creased slightly upward, dimple peeking out ever so slyly as he attempted to steady his breathing. I could tell he was nervous but working hard not to show it; his head held high and body facing straight to the altar. It was almost as if he was worried that he might be distracted if he looked anywhere to his left or right.

By the time the rest of the wedding party walked down the aisle, most of the crowd was standing, turned toward the door and waiting for the bride to enter. But I lingered just a bit longer toward the altar, first at Jake, and then on the groom to see if he was as nervous as everyone else seemed to be. There he stood, running his hands down his tuxedo to straighten it out—and maybe dry off his hands, too—as he prepared to see his bride in her dress for the first time. He definitely was nervous, but his smile had yet to disappear. And within a minute, the Bridal Chorus began playing, and there was Candice, walking down the aisle with her dad, her maid of honor trailing behind to make sure the train on her dress didn't tangle. We could barely keep our eyes off her, but she was gracefully and beautifully only looking at her husband-to-be.

When Candice finally walked up to Lance, her stunning sequined mermaid gown sparkling under the lights, not a dry eye was found in the room.

You could see how clear it was they were meant to be husband and wife. And that? That clarity was something Jake and I never had. We always had the passion and chemistry, but never the certainty. It was what we lacked and what Candice and Lance had in absolute abundance.

I turned to glance at Jake once more and thought I briefly caught him staring back at me. I wasn't quite sure, but with Jake, that was par for the course. He'd say he was in love with me one minute and afraid to commit the next. Instead of dwelling on what might be, I decided to concentrate on what I knew for sure; that he never wanted it to be us standing in front of our friends and family, which meant I needed to move on.

Looking back at the bride and groom, I noticed him hold her trembling hand as they began their vows. "With this ring, I thee wed, and with it, I bestow upon you the treasures of my mind, heart and hands," she said.

I wondered if I'd one day have the same courage as Candice, standing there pledging her heart and body to one man. For the rest of her life. Vowing that her "I" was now permanently a "we" and that she would love this man until the end of her days. Right then, it seemed highly unlikely.

After they exchanged their vows and the wedding party had proceeded out of the room, we walked over to the cocktail reception, the women at the wedding gingerly stepping along so as not to trip in their stilettos or get their heels caught in their dresses. In between laughs and drinking, we struck sly poses to show off what we were wearing. We shifted in our shoes, stuck out our legs and placed hands on our hips, all just to get someone to ask that blessed question: "Where did you get that dress?" What I really wanted to do was place bets on how long each woman would be able to keep her shoes on that night.

I already knew my responses to both, of course. Neiman Marcus for the dress, and one hour, tops, on the shoes. Made of crystal sequins and gold-plated, five-inch heels, they made an impression throughout the room, but they were also *killing* my feet. Unfortunately, I'd committed the cardinal shoe sin of wearing a pair of heels at an event before breaking them in, and I was paying for it. The only upsides were that I knew I had some foldable flats in my purse for later, and, since I was so concentrated on my shoes, they were inadvertently keeping me calm under pressure. So calm, in fact, that I didn't see Jake when he approached a group of us. I was standing around gabbing with some of the girls about the rest of our plans for the weekend when I suddenly heard his voice call my name from behind.

"Rae," he said, using the nickname my parents gave me that most of my close friends had co-opted over time.

I turned around slowly, dreading what was to come next, and there he was, giving me the attention that I'd been waiting for in the ceremony. Jake stood squarely in his black tuxedo and bow tie, with a Tiffany-blue pocket square peeking out, his shoulders just out of reach unless I stood on my tippy toes. His hair was closely shaved down in a low-cut Caesar fade; his five-foot-eleven frame matched only by the smile he had on his face that quite literally lit up the room. *Damn, he looks good.*

"Hey, Reagan." He gave himself just enough time to take my outfit all in as he spoke, but the tension between us was evident from the beginning.

"Hi, Jake," I replied, desperately trying not to focus on him directly.

"You look very beautiful tonight."

"Th-thank you," I stammered. "You look…really nice as well."

"And those shoes. Phew! I see some things never change. You're still rocking the most fire shoes in the whole room."

"Oh, yeah? You like?" I asked, jokingly turning around in a circle to show him the full outfit, but also giving myself a chance to try to remain calm. He was half-right. My *feet* were surely on fire in my shoes, but I didn't plan on letting him or anyone else know that. As I made my turn, I noticed that the women I'd been speaking to had long abandoned me for another conversation, and I couldn't rely on them to get me out of my situation. I had to do it on my own.

"I do, very much." His response, so bold and fast, jolted me out of my thoughts.

By the time I made it back around to him from my circle, he was staring directly into me with an intense glare that snapped away my smile instantly. Jake had a way of doing that, a way that made many of our friends feel uncomfortable when they were around us, like they'd gotten stuck in our bedroom on accident. This time I was just as shocked by the way he could still conjure up such a look for me.

I cleared my throat to keep from buckling under the weight of his eyes on me. "Well, it's good to see you."

Jake said no words in response but reached out his hand to push back the one dark brown curl daring to fall from my loose chignon onto my face, drawing his body even closer to mine. I knew there was only so much longer I could stand in front of him without breaking down and asking all the thoughts that had been running through my head since I saw him walk down that aisle. Things like, "Why not us? Did you ever love me? Do we still have a chance?" I also remembered that he knew me better than anyone, and he could tell my facade was seconds away from giving. The last thing I wanted was for that to happen. Not after he'd made the choice to move and not fight for us.

I stepped back to gain some more space between us.

"You, too," he finally said.

Jake watched me as goose bumps formed on my arms, knowing the exact effect he was having. He stepped back into my space, leaned in and kissed me so softly he barely grazed my skin. His lips landed just off to the side of mine, touching me ever so slightly, but enough to incite chills down my spine. In those few seconds I had time to breathe in his cologne and feel the gentle tickle of the stubble left after shaving his beard. He lingered just long enough to remind me of our first kiss and send signals to my body to go running for the door, get away from everyone and cry. Instead, I closed my eyes and swallowed my tears. When I opened them, I saw him standing in front of me, a slight smirk on his face like he'd won a long-fought battle.

"You know what?" I started before realizing whatever I said wasn't going to be worth it.

"Never mind." I turned around on my crystal heels and left him standing there without as much as a goodbye.

"Wow, this is a real, legit platinum wedding!"

"I know! It's just…wow."

Robin, Jennifer and I overheard a few people commenting on the look of the reception, and we giggled to ourselves. That was the exact reaction we knew our friends wanted when they planned everything. The excited women behind us were right, though, of course. Surrounding us were crystals and sparkles, Tiffany-blue accents and silver trappings. It could almost have been mistaken for an event designed by famed celebrity event planner David Tutera, it was so extravagant.

The place was decadent, but in a good way. Blue-and-silver balloons hung from the ceiling, and each table was adorned with a centerpiece that could have been a chandelier in another lifetime. The decor of the room was only matched by the music and the drinks that were flowing. In fact, the only thing really missing from the wedding was the fourth to our quartet since college, Christine, who was recovering from gall bladder surgery and couldn't make it to Philly. She would have loved every drop of the decadence in the room, and I made a note in my head to remember to take photos so she could see.

For the next hour Jenn, Robin and I took turns dancing to the likes of Stevie Wonder and Bruno Mars, watching Candice and Lance spin around the room to the melodies of their first song, and joining them on the dance floor for Earth, Wind & Fire's "September," the epic ode to love and dancing the night away that had long become a staple at many weddings and Bar Mitzvahs. It was in the midst of all that joy that my feet finally caved to the pain from my Cinderella-style shoes.

I knew it. I knew they wouldn't last more than an hour at this reception.

Luckily, Jenn and Robin seemed to be in the same predicament. After one more quick trot around the dance floor, we looked at each other with knowing glances, and took off in the direction of our table so we could try to seamlessly change into our new shoes for the rest of the evening.

It was like we were in a race. And maybe we were, but only to see who could get relief the fastest. Robin, with her long legs, easily beat me and Jennifer, quickly striding to our table with what seemed like fewer than ten steps. By the time we both sat down to pull our flats out of our purses, she was already remarking how amazing she felt after removing her ankle-strapped, four-inch stilettos.

"Oh, my God, I'm so glad we had the foresight to put our flats in our purses," she sighed, just as Jenn and I plopped down in our seats.

"Are you kidding me? No way we would have

made it without them," Jennifer said. She slid off her right shoe, waving it in the air to us both, before continuing her point: "These things here are pure death traps. Why do we wear them again?"

"Because they look good and we look good in them," I chimed in.

"Oh, right, ha ha, that," Jennifer agreed, laughing. "I guess that does help."

"Mmm-hmm, especially when you want the ex you haven't seen since college to drool over you." Robin cleared her throat as she paused and nodded in my direction, making it very clear her joke was aimed at me.

"Whoop! I think that's you," Jennifer said, slapping me on my thigh as they both cracked themselves up.

"Whatever," I said, rolling my eyes. I wasn't exactly interested in getting into the Jake conversation as we changed into our flats at a dinner table full of people.

"Nah, nah, not whatever. We saw you guys over there being all flirty with each other," Robin said.

"I think anyone with eyes could see that," Jennifer added. She stood up from her seat after sliding on both her shoes, her slender five-foot-six frame suddenly appearing pretty small without the benefit of four-inch heels.

"What you saw was me caught off guard for a second, but nothing more than that. Don't worry."

"So you don't want to see him again tonight?" Jennifer asked.

"I mean… I don't…" I hesitated, trying to find the words to what I'd been feeling for the past few hours without giving them more ammunition for a serious conversation. "Look, all I know is it's been four years since we broke up, and we haven't talked since then. It's a little…hard to see him, that's all."

"You think it's because you still love him?" Jennifer asked.

"I do," Robin jumped in.

"Honestly? I think it's because I'm still hurt that he chose to move after college and didn't fight for us."

"I get that. I do." Jennifer, ever the compassionate foil to Robin's snark, was trying to make me feel better, probably after sensing the conversation was getting a bit too real for our circumstances. "But that doesn't mean you don't want to see him."

"Mmm-hmm, exactly," Robin said, chiming in again. "In fact, I think you better decide quickly if you do because from what I can tell, he's walking up to us in three, two, one…"

Robin stood up as Jake neared our table, her face giving way to any excitement she'd been trying to hold in. Just like earlier in the evening, I looked up and there he was, standing in front of me as I slid my foot into my second flat shoe.

"Rae."

"Jake, we have to stop meeting like this," I said, standing up.

"Ha ha. I guess somehow I do keep sneaking up on you."

"And suddenly, everyone leaves when you come by as well," I said, motioning my hands to show how once again my friends had left me with him.

Jake stepped one foot closer to me.

"I see you took your shoes off," he said, casually changing the conversation.

"Yeah, it was time, but now that I have on my ballet flats, I can properly tear up the dance floor."

I kicked out a leg from underneath my dress to try to break up some of the tension between us, thinking that showing off my flat shoes might lighten the mood.

"Nice," he laughed. "I kinda wish I'd gotten a chance to dance with you in the heels, though."

"Dance with me?" I gave him a quizzical look.

"Yeah, you're not going to save a dance for me?" He smiled like he always did when he was, well, being him. Kind of like the real-life version of a cartoon character who was so charming, a star glistened in one eye when he winked at you.

"Um, sure." I hesitated, realizing I was caught between Jake and the table and couldn't back away. "But why would you need me to have on heels for that?"

"Oh, I don't. I just figured it would've been easier

with you a little taller. Now I might end up stepping all on your dress."

"Ohhhh, you think you're funny. Okay, jerk. I got you." I chuckled and began moving to his side so I could walk away again but was stopped when he grabbed my hand.

"All jokes aside. Reagan Doucet, can I have this dance?"

"Oh, you meant, like, now?"

"Yeah. Now."

He spoke slowly and deliberately, staring daggers into my eyes and melting my resistance under his spell. As soon as our eyes connected, it was like he could read the pages to my inner thoughts with just one look. And once again, he knew it.

"Okay," I breathlessly mouthed before he took my hand in his and walked me to the dance floor, John Legend's "For the First Time" playing in the background.

Walking with one hand in his, I was keenly aware of Robin's and Jenn's eyes on us and also the gentle but firm way he held me, cupping one of my hands in his and his other hand guiding me by the small of my back.

"Do you know how much I've missed you?" he asked as we reached our spot on the dance floor, our eyes once again connecting while I lifted my arms to place them on his shoulders.

"I missed you, too, Jake, but we can't just act like everything's okay between us—"

"I know it's not, Rae, but let's not *but* this evening away, okay?" he said, interrupting me with a
statement that also sort of felt like a plea. "Don't you
miss how good our skin feels together?" His hand
began dragging circles in my palm as he moved one
of my arms from his shoulder to his side. "How our
bodies fit perfectly?" With his other hand still on
my lower back, he pulled me closer to him. "How
our breaths match?"

"I remember," I said, taking in my own deep
breath.

"Then can we just stay in that for now?" Once
again, his eyes poured into mine, cajoling me to do
whatever it was he wanted.

I nodded my head and with a sigh, lowered it and
placed it on his chest as we began dancing to the
music together.

In that moment everything was a blur. I smelled
his cologne and began hearing the smooth sounds of
Luther Vandross and Cheryl Lynn's "If This World
Were Mine." I mouthed the beginning of the song
as if I were part of the duo. It was everything I also
wanted Jake to say so I closed my eyes and pre-
tended he was.

Right before leaving the wedding, a few of us
gathered around Lance and Candice for one last shot
to celebrate them. With our purses and shoes in one
hand, we raised our glasses in the other, ready to
clank them together to mark the occasion.

"To the McCoys!" screamed out the best man.

"To the McCoys!"

I instantly felt hair grow on my chest after downing my shot of whiskey and slammed the glass on the table to try to mask the fact I felt like my insides were burning.

I covered my mouth, coughing, but hoping to still disguise it when I felt a man's hands and arms wrapping around my waist from behind me. I knew it was Jake without even needing to turn around.

"Um, what are you doing?"

"Oh, my bad, is this not allowed?"

"No, it's not allowed," I replied, joking and twisting myself away from his grasp.

"Hmm, just in public or like, period?"

"What are you talking about?" I was genuinely confused about where he was going with the conversation. *Is he drunk?* I wondered. Or maybe taking our moment on the dance floor a bit too far?

"Don't worry about it," he said, changing the conversation and gently pulling me off to the side so we could speak privately. "Can you believe Candice and Lance are married? This stuff's still pretty wild to me."

"I know. It's like, of course they are because they are couple goals, but also, when did we get old enough to be in weddings and watch our friends pledge their lives to each other?"

"For real." He paused. "There's a part of me that always thought it would be us first, though."

"Oh?"

"You didn't?"

I didn't know what to say. Obviously, I'd thought of us being married, but in the time that had passed since we broke up, I'd also worked really hard to get over my heartbreak from him. And there he was trying to pull the Band-Aid off a wound not fully healed yet. "Of course I did, Jake, but—"

"Yeah. I know. Always a *but*," he said, interrupting me and clearly wanting to avoid where our conversation was going. "Hold that thought. I think we need another shot."

I watched him as he ran off to the bar and began telling the bartender exactly what he wanted. Standing somewhat with a nervous energy, I saw him practically instruct her on which drinks to mix, all the while glancing back at me ever so slightly. It wasn't long before he was back before me with four shot glasses in his hands.

"*A* shot, huh?" I laughed nervously.

"Eh, I figured we probably really needed two to take the edge off a bit. Just don't die like you almost did earlier trying to hold in your cough."

"Oh, my God, don't do me like that!"

"Just saying, I thought I was going to have to perform the Heimlich on you or something."

"Whatever. Bring on those shots, jokester." I grabbed my two glasses from him and quickly noticed why he'd been instructing the bartender so much. "You had her make mine Washington Apples?"

"It's still your favorite type of shot, right?"

"It is," I responded with a smile.

"Good. I figured these wouldn't make you cough up a lung and ruin my chances of spending more time with you tonight."

"Oh, boy, somehow I must have forgotten how charming you can be," I said, holding in my giggle. "Let's hurry up and take these shots before I—"

"What, jump on me?" he asked, stepping closer into my space.

"No! Get out of here. In your dreams." I playfully pushed him back a few steps, and we both cracked up laughing.

"All right, all right, you ready?"

"Let's do it."

We'd barely finished our drinks when I looked around and noticed the crowd had dwindled down even more around us, and we were quickly becoming the center of attention. Even Robin and Jennifer were eyeing me with such intensity it felt like the brightest spotlight shining on us, showcasing all my vulnerabilities to everyone still left at the reception.

"Come with me," Jake said, offering his right hand to me and jolting me out of my thoughts.

"I'm sorry, what? Come with you where?"

"Anywhere but here. Just somewhere we can talk and get away from everyone else."

"I don't know if that's a good idea, Jake."

"I know." A smile started to form on his face again. "But come with me anyway."

I titled my head, trying to determine how sincere he was, and then finally gave in and put my hand in his. Without saying another word, he started walking us out of the reception and onto the nearest elevator.

"So that was awkward for you, too, right?" I asked once we were alone.

"Are you kidding me? Our friends are brutal. I thought someone was going to erect a billboard about us while we stood there."

"Yes! Okay, I'm glad I wasn't alone."

"You're never alone when you're with me."

"Stop with the lover-boy moves, please," I said, rolling my eyes and chuckling at the same time.

He laughed. "You know I'm right."

I couldn't help but laugh as well. It was obvious that we were falling right back into the groove we'd had when we were dating, when we could just talk and laugh with each other for hours. In fact, the whole night with him reminded me of our time in college, when we effortlessly just worked, and before he threw it all away.

"That laugh… Damn, I missed that, too," he said as we stepped off the elevator and onto his floor. Still holding my hand, Jake turned to me once more before taking another step in the direction of his room. "I *can* drop you off at your room if that's what you'd rather do. I really was just hoping to spend more time with you, but this has to be your decision."

"No. I'm where I want to be." With my heels off and in my hands, it forced me to look up at him when I talked to him, creating a dynamic that gave him most of the power. The tricky part was I was all too ready to give in to him, the feminist in me be damned.

"Good."

With the answer he'd been waiting for, we walked down the hallway until we reached his hotel room, pausing just long enough to give me a chance to view it from his opened door. Like mine, it featured crisp white curtains flanking the widest windows I'd seen in a hotel before, and modern black-and-red furniture that provided a sleek getaway from the glitz and glam happening downstairs. But he also had a view of Philadelphia that was way more impressive than mine. It was striking just how beautiful it was, and I found myself staring out the window for a beat.

As if he could read my mind, Jake came up behind me and whispered, "You're even more beautiful, you know."

"I'm sure you say that to all the girls."

"Nah, just to you."

"Jake."

"I'm serious! Well, okay, obviously, I've said it to other girls before, but Rae, I meant it when I said I haven't been able to stop thinking about you lately. And then seeing you tonight, it all makes sense. We make sense."

My back facing him, his whispers conveniently hit right behind my ear, sending shivers down my spine. I was almost certain my knees buckled, giving me away, so I turned to face him and give myself a chance to stand straight again.

"I get that," I said, staring into the same eyes that had pulled the truth out of me on so many occasions in the past. "I always thought we were a perfect fit."

"We still can be, you know."

He leaned down and kissed me, our lips intertwining and breaths syncing up as we pulled each other closer. Instantly, I was swept into the moment and released a sigh of pleasure as I gave in to him and to my own desires. Putting up zero resistance, I melted into Jake's embrace as he dragged his hand from the nape of my neck to my back and slowly released the zipper from my gown. Then he swung me back around toward the window and began kissing my neck and spine and lower back as he made his way down, the dress falling with him. By the time he was done, I was standing only in my bra and panties and ballet flats, the dress gathered at my ankles.

"Wow," he whispered, his eyes following the length of my body. "Touching is allowed now, yes?"

I chuckled and stepped out of the dress to fully reveal myself—pink panties, pink bra, pink flats and brown skin. "Uh-huh. Very much so."

Without another word, he picked me up, laid me down on his bed and slid my underwear off in what felt like one fell swoop.

"You belong to me for the next few hours. Is that all right?"

He focused his eyes on mine again, waiting for my

response, alternating sliding one hand down the side of my body and the other tracing the lips on my face.

"Mmm-hmm."

"Say yes or I'll stop."

"Yes." Slowly, I saw him stand up and begin to take his suit off, piece by piece—first his tie, then his jacket, shirt, pants and finally his boxer briefs. This time I got to marvel at him; the way his shoulders rose up and down with his breathing, the vee-cut at his hips that led your eyes to his penis, the way it jumped when he caught me admiring him.

And with that same smirk and dimple peeking out again, he walked back to the bed, draping his body on mine, and took my lips into his.

Four hours later I awoke in Jake's bed, the light from his phone flickering on and off from texts he was getting throughout the night. I turned my head, trying to drown out the light and focus on the fact that he had his arms wound tightly around me. Our breaths were still in sync, too; our chests rising and falling on beat with each other. What did this all mean? I wondered as I felt him pull me tighter to him even as he slept. Was this the start of us getting back together? Had I misjudged him before? Was this his way of saying he was ready to fight for us now?

His phone light shone again from the nightstand. *Who could this be?* I thought, finally unable to resist checking. I leaned over, slightly releasing myself from his grip, and pressed the phone screen to drag the notifications down and see what the messages said. In an instant I found myself in the middle of a group chat with some of his best friends.

Hey, you still with Reagan?

Come on Fred, u know he is.

Guess he couldn't pass that old thing up, huh?

Wonder what Shannon would think about that.

Ohhh snap! She definitely wouldn't like that.

Man, don't listen to these fools. Hit us up when you done.

What? Horrified, I read on as each message threw me a new gut punch. Not only were his friends talking about me as just some "old thing" to have sex with, Jake maybe also had a girlfriend named Shannon? At the very least, she was someone they all knew who had the right to be upset about Jake and me together. It was too much to take in. I closed my eyes, trying to drown out what I'd just read, hoping it would somehow make it not real. After a few seconds I opened them again and checked. *Nope. Still there. I should have known.*

My head began to spin as reality came crushing down. He had only asked if I could be his for the next few hours, I remembered. And he'd never once said anything about us getting back together. Just that he missed me, and clearly wanted to have sex. But he had to have known that I would want more, right? *Ugh. How could I have been such an idiot? He's a man; why did I just assume this was anything more than sex?*

I slid out of bed so as not to wake him and caught the tears as they were just about to start coming down my face. No. He wouldn't get the pleasure of me crying again. Not this time. And I certainly didn't want to look him in his face again and have him break my heart once more. I grabbed my things from the floor—my bra, underwear, purse, flats, dress and finally my heels—and began putting my bra and then dress on.

I had to get out of there as soon as I could. With my dress halfway zipped up, I walked out of his room, vowing to never be that stupid for him or anyone else, ever again.

Chapter One

October 28, 2019

It was barely 7:00 a.m. when I heard my alarm blasting the sounds of Nicki Minaj's "Pound the Alarm."

"Not yet, Alexa." Groggy and yearning for at least five more minutes of sleep, I stretched my arm over the length of my bed and pressed down on the snooze button with my eyes still closed. It wasn't that I didn't want to get up, necessarily; it was just that the cocoon of my comforter in my queen-size bed felt so much better than whatever could have been waiting for me outside it. I pulled the cover over my head as an extra protection against the sun.

"Pound the alarm!"

"Agh!" I screamed out as it went off once more. "Fine, fine. I'm up now."

The music still blaring, I finally acquiesced and rolled myself out of bed, one leg coming free from my cover cocoon, then the next, and made my way to my closet for what had become my daily routine: pick out shoes for the day, figure out the outfit that goes best with them, take a shower and then, of course, post my #shoeoftheday photo to Instagram before heading to work. Conveniently, I passed right over the red pumps that spelled disaster for me the night before.

"Hmm, now what do I feel like wearing today?" I questioned, dancing to my closet and scanning all the shoes I own with my eyes, from my flats to my heels, boots to sneakers, in every color one can imagine. They were all intricately displayed on the shelves— heels facing out to show the length and style of the pump, flats facing forward to make it easier for me to see if it was a peep toe, curved toe, pointed toe or square.

"Oooh, these!" Something about my deep red, almost maroon peep-toe heels from BCBG caught my eyes, and I knew they were the ones for the day. The shoes were adorned with a silver buckle on the side of each peep toe and would go perfectly with my red-and-pink floral blouse, black pencil skirt and peplum blazer to match. It was amazing how the rest of an outfit could come together for me once I picked out the shoes, and today was no exception. These might even be the ones to help me finally convince my boss to let me do the article I'd been pitching to him for months. Excited about my choices, I laid them out on my bed and hopped in the shower, continuing my best rap impressions as my playlist toggled through my favorite female rappers.

It was 9:00 a.m. when I walked into work at Washington, DC's premier political news online magazine, my heels clacking on the linoleum floors they must have purchased just to make it that much easier for women to alert everyone of their comings and goings in the office. Seated at her desk already was my always-early, no-holds-barred freckle twin, and the best IT specialist in the office, Rebecca, her reddish-blond hair pulled up into a loose bun and a smile on her face the size of a kid in a candy store.

"So…" she said, dragging out her first word. "Tell me about last night."

"Oh, my God, let me sit down first before I embarrass myself, please." Adding on the extra drama, I slid my hand across my face like a diva in an old Hollywood movie.

Rebecca blinked, curious of what could have happened in the ten hours since she'd seen me. "Wait, what? When we talked at happy hour last night, you had a whole plan to seduce 'ol' boy.'" She was careful to use the moniker we'd long ago decided to call any of the guys I dated since they usually didn't last long enough for my friends to remember their names.

"Oh, I'm aware," I said, finally sitting in my chair at my desk, conveniently located next to hers. "But let's just say things didn't go as planned."

"Okay, now you really have to tell me what happened. Is the man not seducible?"

"Ha! No, that's not it." I stopped myself. "I'm sure he's very seducible. I, however, may not be the one to try it again."

I paused for a second to turn on my computer and see if any emails were in my inbox, especially from either Peter, my boss, or any of the leads I'd been working on for the story I wanted to pitch to him. *Damn, not one. Just more of the same junk as always.* As my main act of defiance, work-life balance, or both, in the four years I'd worked there, I'd yet to put my emails on my phone, so my mornings usually consisted of me catching up on details in my inbox and gabbing with Becs.

I rolled my chair closer to her desk after I'd finished my quick scan so I could give her all the juicy details somewhat privately. "All right, he comes over last night looking so sexy," I recounted, beginning my story and halfway reminding myself how well the evening had started. "He's wearing gray sweatpants, so you know he knows what's up, smelling like YSL cologne, standing tall with his broad shoulders that make you just want to jump into his arms, those stunningly beautiful green eyes and of course, his man bun sitting perfectly on top of his head."

Rebecca pushed her chair even closer to mine,

fully captivated and ready to hear the rest. "Mmm-hmm."

I spanned the office once more to see who all was around yet. Thankfully for us, it was still fairly empty. Most of the people in our office casually strolled in on a good day around 10:00/10:30 a.m., but Rebecca was an early bird, and I couldn't live down the reminder my parents always gave me as a kid: "You have to be twice as good to get half as far, Rae." That meant neither of us ever arrived later than 9:00 a.m. It was part of what had bonded us four years ago when I started.

I continued, "I answer the door, trying to be all Jessica Rabbit-like, letting him take in my lingerie. And you can tell he's into it. I catch his eyes roaming all up and down my body, so I'm just standing there letting him do it, like yeah."

Rebecca laughed.

"It doesn't take long before we're in my room. We're kissing, he's grabbing my hair, I'm holding on to his back, everything is going just how I wanted. Until he almost trips on my red pumps by the bed," I said, hanging my head in shame.

"Wait, why were they by the bed? I thought you were going to wear them when you opened the door?"

"I was, but then last minute I realized, I'm not fully that girl, so I tossed them off by my bed," I said, laughing. "Anyway, he's like, 'What are these doing here?' picking them up and mocking me with them. 'I know Reagan doesn't keep her shoes any-where but her sacred shoe closet,' he says. 'What, were you planning to seduce me or something?'"

"Well, he's not wrong."

"Whatever." I rolled my eyes before continuing on with the story. "Can you imagine how embarrass-ing this was, Becs? Not only did I change my mind on doing that, now he's calling me out on it? Ugh! If only it didn't get worse."

"Oh, damn, girl. Worse?" Rebecca's face has al-ready turned red from the thought of what could have gone wrong.

"Exactly. So now I'm trying to save face, and I'm all, 'How about you put those down, lie down and just let me take over.'"

"My girl. I see you!"

"Ha ha, don't be too impressed yet," I reminded her, using my hand to calmly bring down her energy from a ten to a two. "He lies down on the bed, and I start doing my thing—swaying my hips from side to side, winding my body down to almost a squat just to bring it back up. I drag my hands down my body, lingering on my breasts before making their way to my stomach and then my thighs. Like, I'm in *control*, okay?"

"Okay!" Rebecca chimed in again, still waiting for the embarrassing part.

"And he is just lying there, paralyzed into submis-sion on the bed, watching me turn myself on. Want-ing to move so badly, but not wanting the show to end, right? I do this for about ten minutes, and before he can get up, I drop down to my knees once more, turn back around and crawl my way up his body. I'm sliding my breasts up his legs, making sure they touch him just enough to tease him but not enough for him to fully feel their impact. And finally, I decide I'm going to do one more move. I wink at him, get up and wind my body around one more time, finally unhooking the back of my bra, letting the strap of one side down and then the other, and watching him watch me as gravity drops the bra out of sight and leaves my breasts in full view."

"Rae, I think we need to have a talk about the definition of *embarrassing*."

"Wait for it," I reminded her again. "Now, he's still lying there, and I can feel his desire oozing off of him. I swing my right leg out to kick the bra off the bed. And then, wham!"

"Oh, no!"

"Oh, yes," I confirmed, nodding to show it really did happen. "I fell. Lost my footing, tripped on the bra and went flailing over the side of the bed. Falling in the least sexy way possible. In slow motion. Backward. And onto those damn red heels."

Mimicking my fall, I slid down in my chair, but caught myself before I actually fell onto the floor. Pencil skirts weren't made for getting up off the ground, I chided myself.

"Ohhhhh nooooo."

"Yep."

"Oh, my God, Rae. What did he do?"

"Oh, that's the worst part! He laughed! He legit sat up and cracked up laughing at me on the floor."

"You've got to be kidding me."

"Nope. Unfortunately, I am not."

"What did you do?"

"I stood up eventually and kicked him out. Like, what? Okay, it was probably really funny, but make sure I'm okay first before you just start howling with laughter," I said, half laughing and half shaking my head. Rebecca joined in as the image of me falling off the bed hit her again. "Needless to say, that one is over."

"Yeah, I sort of figured by the end of the story he was."

"That's what, the fourth guy this year now that's made it past the first date and still ended up being a bust? Becs, seriously. There's got to be more than *this* out there, right?"

"Of course, honey, this was just one for the books," she replied. "But there's so many fish in the sea. This is just a blip and a funny story in your basically perfect life."

"Bleh, it's definitely not perfect," I groaned. "And I know, he's just a blip, but damn, I date all the time, and like, nothing. It always ends in some foolishness."

"I get that, but are we going to be honest here? Because it's not like you really invest in these guys anyway. Yeah, you date *a lot*." Rebecca emphasized her last words by punctuating them with air quotation marks. "But you already know going in they are either not trying to do anything serious or they want to marry you tomorrow, which makes you feel instantly smothered."

"But don't you think that's crazy that's the pattern? What's a girl gotta do to get something in the middle?"

"Hmm. Maybe risk opening up to one of these guys and seeing if it can actually be something more?"

"Bleh." Even coupled with Becs's best older sister look, I was completely not interested in that idea. "Just call me 'five-month Betty,' I guess. I keep 'em for five months, and then I'd rather just focus on my shoe-of-the-day posts online and work on convincing Peter to let me write about the ways women are shaping the world of politics instead of having to write yet again about how the Republicans and Democrats aren't getting along in Congress."

"One, five-month Betty is hilarious and might be your new nickname now," Rebecca laughed. "Two, Peter loves you and everything you do, so I'm sure it won't take that much convincing."

"You say that, and all y'all think that and yet, every week I'm stuck still writing the same thing. Don't get me wrong, I get paid a lot, so I'm not *really* complaining, but like how many times can you write the same thing over and over? We get it. They don't like each other!"

"Three," Rebecca continued, undeterred from my interruption, "you are definitely doing your thing with those shoe-of-the-day posts. What do you have, like fifteen thousand followers now?"

"It's actually seventeen," I corrected her, jokingly patting the bottom of my hair in response. "And yet, I'm also the same girl who was ghosted by the last guy the day after we'd talked about me helping him prepare for his open mic and then had the next one not understand the rules of laughing at someone."

Rebecca raised her arms to pretend as if she was playing a tiny violin. "Oh, poor Rae," she said, winking to let me know she was at least somewhat messing with me. "Sounds to me like you need to listen to some more Megan Thee Stallion today or something. Get your energy back up."

In the distance we heard another pair of heels on the linoleum floor, prompting Rebecca to scooch a little back to her desk but stop in her tracks when she heard the shoes turn off to the right, away from us. At almost 9:30 a.m., we knew it was likely the Black woman in the general counsel office, her routine similar to ours.

The coast clear, Rebecca added, "Then, we can continue this conversation."

"You may be correct."

"Oh, I am. You can't let 'ol boy' and those red pumps get you down this much. You did enough of that last night," she muttered under her breath, chuckling at her joke.

"Oh, God, I'm never living this down, am I?"

"Yeah, probably not any time soon."

Defeated in getting her to join me in my attempt at having a woe-is-me moment, I rolled my chair back to my desk and scrolled through the emails in my inbox again.

Mueller report, congresswoman resigns after sex scandal, impeachment inquiry…

Damn, it was a depressing morning.

"I see Peter coming down the hallway, so now might be as good a time as any to catch him," Rebecca said, interrupting my thoughts. She was the perfect spy at our job, especially for Peter. Somehow, her desk was positioned just so that she could see him when he was anywhere near his office, and yet, he could not see her. I checked my watch and noticed the time: 10:00 a.m. Just like clockwork.

"Good looking out, Becs." I stood up from my chair and smoothed out my skirt, checking out the floor to see where he was in relation to his office. If I left then, I could meet him at his office door as he walked up to it and command his attention before the day got too busy.

"Good luck!" Rebecca whisper-screamed out as I *click-clacked* past her. Peter's office was only a few feet away, which meant it took me only a minute to catch up to him. He was, as was typical, preoccupied in his phone, likely checking to see what news he'd have to manage for the day.

"Peter!" I practically screamed as he walked up,

realizing only too late that my enthusiasm was probably a bit too much. For better or for worse, he barely recognized it.

"Oh, hi, Reagan, just the person I wanted to see. Have a seat," he said, pointing to one of the chairs in his office as we walked in. He barely let me sit down before he started talking. "Now, as I'm sure you've seen, Representative Linda Frasier announced her resignation yesterday. I put something on the front page over the weekend that just covered the breaking news aspect, but I know you've been wanting to do more articles about women and politics, and this might be the place to try it."

I could hardly stop myself from rolling my eyes. *Wow, what a concept*, I thought. Finally talking about the challenges that women face in politics only after the Democratic congresswoman who is accused of having improper relationships with staffers resigns, but not when I initially wanted to discuss the ugliness of her intimate photos being released to the public. *Why was I here again?*

"I know, I know," Peter continued, completely oblivious to the ways I was biting my tongue as he spoke. "This isn't exactly what you were hoping for, but I'd still love to see what you can do with it."

"Oh," I blurted out before I could stop myself. "What exactly were you looking for?"

"I don't know yet, Reagan. I'm hoping you can tell me. There's a part of me that feels like we've beat this drum to death. Everyone's done stories about representatives having illicit affairs for decades now. But you told me you could do something different with it, right?"

"Yes, I did." It was moments like this with Peter when I appreciated being at a job with a boss who liked my work. He didn't always get it right; he had tons of blind spots as an early 40s white man from Maine who thought he was super liberal, but well... wasn't, but this was the kind of opportunity he dangled in front of me like a carrot, and I was all too ready to jump for it.

"I mean, you're right, it's not *exactly* what I've been pitching, but if it gets me closer to that, I'll take it."

"Okay, great." Peter smiled, feeling his own sense of satisfaction from the conversation. "Now, was there something you wanted to talk about?"

"Uhhh, no. Just, when do you want the pitch?"

"Sooner the better. If I like it, I'd like to run it by the end of the week."

"Done." I stood up to leave his office but stopped before walking out. "Thanks again, Peter. You won't regret it."

"I know," he said. "Just don't make it about race, okay? Linda Frasier is a white woman who resigned because she was having affairs with white staffers. I know you're interested in this intersectionality thing, but let's see how this one goes first." He didn't even raise his head when he said it. Of course, if I just kept the story strictly about Rep. Frasier, focusing on the intersectionality of different forms of oppression wouldn't play an important role, but it hadn't been my intention to do so.

Putting on my brave face, I practically skipped back to my desk to mask the disappointment Rebecca was bound to notice if I didn't. It wasn't that she wouldn't be compassionate if I told her what happened; it's just that the last thing I wanted to do was talk to someone about it at that moment. Instead, I acted like I'd gotten everything I wanted.

"Be careful. We don't know if there are any red pumps lying around," Rebecca laughed as she saw me bouncing back to our desks.

"I'm so done with you right now," I laughed, plopping down in my chair and taking it for a spin. I was really putting on a show; one would never have known the thing I wanted to do the most was lay my head on my desk and break out into an ugly cry.

"I told you Peter loved you and everything you do," Rebecca said, turning back to her desk. "I can't wait to see this new article at the top of the site."

"Okay, okay, you may be right about that one thing," I joked.

"I've got eight years on you, dear Rae. I'm right about a whole lot more than one thing."

Sometimes you can tell how a day will end by the way that it begins. If the birds are practically singing with you down the street on your way to the Metro like you're freakin' Snow White, chances are pretty good that the day will be roses and sunshine throughout. But what about when you've been holding back tears since the alarm blared and you walked past the bright red symbols of your loneliness? That day probably won't end well.

It was 3:43 p.m. when I saw Robin's number on my office phone, not normally the number she would call if she just had a funny story to tell midday. Hesitant to pick it up, I let it ring a few times before I pulled my headphones out of my ears and grabbed the receiver.

"Hey, Robin, what's up?"

"Do you have a moment?" I heard her words but more importantly, her tone, and knew something was wrong.

"Sure."

"It's about Christine. She's been admitted to the hospital again."

"Oh, no." I felt my head get light but tried to concentrate on what she was saying.

"And this time her organs are starting to fail, so her mom asked me to call everyone and let them know what is going on."

"What do you mean her organs are starting to fail?" I could feel the dread growing inside me with every word Robin said. Christine and I had been friends since high school in New Orleans and both decided to go to college in DC, so she'd been with me through every significant moment for the past eleven years. It was her wild and crazy self that helped bring our quartet together—Christine, the raspy, speak-her-mind-at-all-times Afro-Latina who randomly, and often unconsciously, tossed in Spanish words as she spoke; Robin, the snarky but actually sort of sweet-at-heart girl from the Midwest; Jennifer, the compassionate one from sunny California who wore her heart and everyone else's on her sleeves; and me, the shoe fanatic who loved laughing, hated crying and always wanted to be the strong friend for everyone. Even as we'd all grown up and started our own careers, we stayed close, making sure to see each other at least once a week to catch up on the details of our lives. And now Christine's organs were failing? *In what universe was that okay?* I thought.

"You know she's been having these complications since her gallbladder surgery," Robin said, bringing me back into the phone conversation.

"Yeah, I know, but even after all her hospital visits, her organs never started failing." With tears threatening to pour down my face, I bit my tongue again, even as I tried to get as much information out of Robin as I could. "I mean, what does that even mean?"

"It's her lungs," she relented. "Her mom says they're not functioning properly."

I was silent. Numb even. A million thoughts raced through my head and then all stopped at one: Christine was going to die. Her lungs. That was all I could hear Robin say, *People definitely needed lungs to live.*

"The doctors are doing what they can to get them

back working again, but I mean, you know when the organs start failing—"

I interrupted her, not wanting to hear the actual words. "I know, I know." My head began pounding, because it wasn't enough that I felt light-headed and had the deepest desire to slink down under my desk and never be seen again. I also apparently needed a headache on top of everything. On top of my best friend dying.

"I'm probably going to leave work in a few to go see her," Robin continued over the phone. "I don't think I'm going to be able to concentrate until I do."

"Yeah," I replied, not really knowing what other words to say and holding my forehead with one hand while I gripped the phone with the other. "I'll call you back in a little bit. Let me check with Peter to see if I can leave, too. This is the last place I want to be right now."

"No problem." Robin paused. "Hey, Reagan?"

"Yeah."

"I just want you to know that I love you." Her voice was filled with worry and concern, and you could tell she'd been crying.

"I love you, too, Robin," I said. "I love you, too."

I hung up the phone and stared at the ceiling for a brief moment before my feet had a mind of their own and my *click-clacks* ran through the hallway to the bathroom. Locking the door behind me, I stood facing myself in the mirror, holding back the tears so desperate to come out.

"It can't be her time yet," I said aloud. "It just can't be." I slumped down onto the counter, my legs no longer able to hold my weight up, and felt my thighs hit the cold, hard floor. It was no use in worrying about my pencil skirt when my world was falling apart. I vaguely heard Rebecca outside the door, asking if I was okay, but my mouth couldn't move to answer her.

Chapter Two

Bright and early on a Saturday morning, I found myself in a swanky gym locker room, less than a fifteen-minute walk from my apartment. Robin, Jenn and I had spent the past week sitting beside Christine's bed more than anywhere else, but in desperate need of a distraction, I'd agreed to join Rebecca at a morning spin class at our local gym. And while I'd jumped at the chance to do something, anything really, other than think about Christine's drip-drop slow recovery, it dawned on me not too soon after I met up with her that there was one small problem with me agreeing to the class: I hated spin.

Like, literally hated everything about it. It wasn't that I didn't think it could help; I knew a lot of people who swore by its health benefits, and certainly knew I'd be guaranteed to have an hour off from worrying. But over the years, spinning had become almost cult-like with its many variations, such as Soul Cycle, Trap Cycle and how could I forget the one that claimed it felt more like working out in a nightclub? Beyond even that, the thing I disliked most about spin was the way my butt felt during the class. Everyone always said that eventually your butt gets used to the feeling of the bike, but when I'd tried it before… Nah.

Regardless, there I was, putting on my spin sneakers on the wood-grain floors, marveling at the rotation of women coming in and out of the doors, looking like the exact models you might expect to see in spin class ads: blond hair tied in either a loose high ponytail or twirled in an up-do that took thirty minutes to do, but seemed effortless; Lululemon workout gear, S'well water bottles and enough sweat that they glistened, but not so much where they were actually drenched. I glanced up to see if Rebecca looked as nervous as I felt.

"Are you sure we're ready for this?" I asked, trying to give us one last shot at running away.

"Ha, yes, I'm sure." She paused. "I mean, kind of sure."

I could sense her hesitation. Maybe she, too, was worried that we weren't really the duo that fit in with the rest of the spin-bots before us? Even if we did have some things in common with them.

"You know our butts are going to be on fire afterward, right?" I asked, anxiously making sure the pink Velcro on my turquoise-and-white sneakers was fully snapped closed so that the shoes didn't become a death trap for me on the bike pedals.

"Yeah, I know." Rebecca's once assured voice had been replaced with a nervous chuckle, and I remembered exactly why we were friends. Neither of us felt entirely comfortable where we were, but we were going to try it together. "But we've tried other things before, and it worked out. I'm sure this will be fine. Remember when we did Zumba this summer for a couple months? That was fun!"

"Zumba was fun—wait, why did we stop going there again?"

"Umm, great question," she said, walking over to the water fountain to fill her own S'well water bottle. "Honestly, I think it's because we just didn't make the time for it. Who wants to go to Zumba when there's happy hours, right?"

"That's facts," I joked. "But this is different. Spin is…" I rubbed a butt cheek just thinking of how it felt previously and lost track of my sentence. "I just quickly found out last time I tried that I didn't have as much cushion in my tushion as I thought back then."

"Your tushion?"

"Yeah, my tushion! That's how much I thought I was packing behind me, but it wasn't enough."

The thought caused us both to laugh, one of those good, loud, from-your-stomach kind of laughs. It was the first one I'd had since getting Robin's call, and it felt good to have that feeling come through me again, even it meant enduring an hour of physical pain.

"First of all, that was like five or six years ago, so I'm guessing some things have improved since then. Second, you know you have more cushion in front of you than behind you," she added, making reference to the double-D breasts I'd acquired while gaining a few pounds over the years. I loved when Rebecca started making her points with numbers. It meant she was really invested in you listening to what she had to say. Unfortunately for her, it usually just caused me to chuckle inside, which was kind of the exact opposite reaction I'm guessing she wanted. "But," she continued, "even if neither of those things were true, we'd still push through. That's what we do."

I admired her tenacity, especially since I knew inside, she was just as concerned as I was, but was likely trying her best to be a good friend to me. Guess that meant it was my turn to stop complaining and join her in carrying the load of us having fun that morning.

"I sure hope so," I replied with a wink and then remembered one important fact I needed to correct her on. "But hey, don't hate, you know my butt is surprisingly very firm."

Rebecca rolled her eyes and shook her head at me. "All right, bootylicious. Yes, how could I forget? Now, let's get out of here before we're late."

We gathered up our items and slid them into our lockers, double-checking that we remembered our combination codes on the locks before clicking the doors closed. I turned to her once more, as we scooped up our water bottles and towels and began walking to our spin class like we were pros. It was clear she wanted to probe but wasn't sure if she should.

"How is Christine doing, by the way?" she finally blurted out. "Any better?"

"Not really." I fidgeted, not knowing how much I could talk about it without breaking down, but also wanting to be sensitive to her needs as a friend as well. I moved the water bottle to under my arm as we walked up to the classroom, needing something to do with my hands. "She's sort of touch and go, but still fighting to get out of the hospital."

"Okay," she said. "I know you don't want to talk about it, but I had to ask at least once."

"I get it."

The instructor was standing at the front of the classroom when we walked in, her enthusiasm leaping off her.

"Hi there," she nearly squealed out. "I'm Kelly, and we're so excited to see some new people join us today. I hope you enjoy yourself, and let me know if you need any help getting yourself set up."

"Thanks, Kelly!" we both said in unison, walking past her. "We hope so, too."

"And what about you? How are you handling everything?" Rebecca turned to watch me as she spoke, briefly halting our pursuit of a set of bikes next to each other.

"Becs, honestly…" I paused to get my thoughts together. "I'm mostly focused on being there for her. Obviously, you naturally start wondering if you're doing everything you should be doing while you have time on this earth. But I really haven't had the time to go there. As you know, this is the first thing I've done outside of going to the hospital and work in a week."

"Maybe you should be thinking about that, too, though," she suggested. "That's not you being self-ish. It's just remembering to take care of yourself."

"Yeah, maybe," I said, pausing again. "I guess I have been sort of wondering, like, if I died tomorrow, could I say I was really happy before then?"

She blinked a few times at my honesty, but also wanted to make sure she understood me correctly. "You mean, do you do enough?"

"No, I mean do I spend too much time trying to do everything I *think* I should?"

"Oh, now that's a great question, Rae."

Rebecca placed her hand on my shoulder and gave me a knowing nod that spoke volumes to what she believed my answer to the question would be. She wanted to dig in more, but she also knew I'd agreed to spin that morning to get away from having to think about death and the consequences of spending your life focused on other people's standards. After a few silent seconds she turned back around to restart our bike pursuit, noticing that more people were walking into the class and picking out their own bikes.

We spent the next couple minutes scoping out our perfect location: next to the window, not quite in front, but definitely not all the way in the back. This way we could see the instructor and be seen, but not find ourselves in front of the entire class. Then we began the grueling process of making sure the bikes we picked were perfectly adjusted for us, something that comes much more easily the longer one takes a spin class. Since we were new-ish, however, it took us a bit of time. We struggled raising the seat, felt out of place trying to measure how our legs felt on the pedals, and tried out the handles standing and sitting. Even after we finally felt like we had everything adjusted, we checked again. The last thing either of us wanted was to realize halfway through the class that we were too far away from the handles, and we'd made the hills even harder for us to climb.

With one last check and an extra look from Kelly, we were both finally ready. Well, as ready as we could be. I felt my butt one more time and apologized to it again for the torture that I was about to inflict on it, hopped back onto my bike and slid my new sneakers into the straps, getting myself into position.

As soon as we were locked and ready, waiting for Kelly to begin, Rebecca leaned toward me, hoping she could put a nice pin on the tail end of our conversation.

"So," she said, "you think this means you're ready to put down your life to-do checklist and just figure out what makes you happy?"

A little caught off guard, I turned my head to her and squinted my eyes. *I thought we were done with this*, I thought. *But I guess not.* Seeing no way to avoid her question, I responded, "Don't act like there's not something extremely gratifying about checking off items on a to-do checklist. Don't hate," I halfway joked. "But maybe something like that. I don't know. Christine is always saying how I live a 'cautious life,' so maybe it's just doing more things outside my comfort zone."

Kelly cleared her throat, her passive-aggressive way of letting us know that class was about to begin, and waited for everyone to go silent and look in her direction before she turned on her first piece of music.

"Are you guys ready for a great class?" she called out to the room full of bikers, effectively, at least briefly, interrupting our conversation. "We'll be doing a combination of cardio and strength today, so I hope you're ready to work."

She scanned her attention around the class and waited for each person to nod before moving on to the next. When she stopped in my direction, it fully felt as if she was asking me the question personally. So I nodded just like the others. It was time to get the bike party started.

As we began climbing our fake hills, I couldn't stop thinking of the idea of a "cautious life." As much as Christine had chided me on it over the years, I'd always been able to come back at her with the truth of how we were both brought up: you follow the straight and narrow path, you get the results you want. You go to college and work hard, you come out and get the high-paying job you want. That motto then turned into: you date enough people, you'll eventually meet the person you're going to spend the rest of your life with. Spend time with your friends, and you'll have the perfect *Sex and the City*–like life with brunches and happy hours and all the shoes you could ever desire. Check, check and check. By the time we'd be done talking, she was on my side.

So why does it feel like all my accomplishments are holding on by a thread? My best friend who traipsed with me to every happy hour under the sun is in the hospital. I've dated more men than I can count and still haven't found "the one" and I am in a job that people wished for but sometimes made me want to pull my eyelashes out one at a time.

As if Rebecca could read my thoughts, she turned her head to me again. We were just beginning to pick up the pace on our bikes, and the burn in our calves was ever so slightly coming in.

"What do you think about doing a different kind of list?" she asked.

"Huh?" I was equal parts lost in my own thoughts and vividly realizing how long it had been since I worked out, so I'd barely processed her question.

"Like a list to help you break out of your comfort zone."

"Tell me more," I said, jumping back into my skin

and hoping the conversation would distract from the pain jutting into my legs and butt cheeks.

"What if you made a list of things that you only consider in those quiet moments at home in your shoe closet, and then went about actually doing them?"

"Like a risk list?" I asked, my breath getting heavier as the hill became harder to climb.

"Yes!" she screamed out before realizing how loud she was. "Yessss," she whispered this time around, giving Kelly the my-bad look kids give when they do something like break a glass or accidentally pull down everything on your dresser. "Exactly that."

We eased up on our bikes a bit as we began going downhill. This was normally the time in the spin class when you had a moment to catch your breath, but Kelly wasn't letting up. I couldn't tell if she was always that evil or just adding a little extra because of the two chatty Cathys on the side of her classroom.

"Let's add some speed now that we're back on a flat road!" Sweat began pouring down my face as if it had been waiting for her to give it permission. *I was certainly not glistening like the ladies we saw in the locker room earlier.* I focused my attention back on my pedaling, the fast pace ensuring me that whatever else Rebecca wanted to talk about would have to wait. She was undeterred, however. Huffing and puffing, she leaned in once more.

"And while you're thinking about adding things to the list," she said then hesitated again. "I wonder if you might want to finally reach out to Jake to talk about what happened at the wedding."

Stunned and barely able to breathe, I spun my head around to showcase my displeasure.

"Wait, what? How did we go from Christine and a risk list to Jake?" I was completely confused but somehow able to pant out my response.

"I don't know. I've just been thinking," Rebecca said, shrugging. "You were talking about how awful dating has been lately and it might be because you never resolved that situation."

"That has nothing to do with Jake, Becs."

"Doesn't it have everything to do with him?"

In the background I heard "Over It" by Katharine McPhee begin playing on Kelly's speaker. *How apropos.*

"I mean, I still can't get that image of you running from his room out of my head," she continued while trying to whisper. "You tripped and everything, trying so desperately to get away from that man!"

"You know how hurt I was in that moment," I said, no longer even wanting to look at her for bringing up Jake. *This was supposed to be my time away from everything.*

"I know. But don't you think you've been taking the safe route ever since that relationship blew up in your face?"

"Twice," I reminded her. I may have been unable to breathe, but I knew all too well how much that relationship had hurt me.

"Yes, it blew up twice," Rebecca replied, her big-sister voice attempting to lull me further into a discussion I had no desire to be in. "So I get it. All you can remember now are the hurtful times between y'all. But if you really want to make a change, it starts with having a real talk with Jake. It's time."

Huge globs of sweat poured down both our faces as we attempted to one up each other in the conversation. It was a foolish plan, but we'd both entered that part of a girl-talk moment where neither of us was willing to back down.

"Listen, I can't be focused on Jake now. I need to concentrate on getting back in top shape, getting these thighs to come down from this size ten back to an eight. On being there for Christine, her family and our friends. Hell, even doing this risk list we were *just* talking about. There's no time for me to add him in the midst of all that."

I exhaled as we entered into an even higher-speed portion of the spin class, drawing breaths from some place magical inside me.

"Okay, Reagan, I hear you, but it just sounds like you're still running scared out of that room, except that it's in your head now. And with Christine in the hospital, I just don't want—"

I could tell the class was beginning to get hard for Rebecca, too, because her last sentence included an intake of breath after almost every word. It gave me the perfect opportunity to jump in before she could finish.

"No, I'm being smart," I whispered back defiantly. "Can we just focus on spin for now, please? We're getting dirty looks as it is."

"Sure. For now." Rebecca shrugged again and gave Kelly another "sorry" expression as her once polite and perky face had turned to that of a stern instructor clearly upset at us for talking through the length of her class. "I won't push it more."

"Thank you. Plus, there are a million reasons why we could never work," I said, attempting to get the last word.

"I said okay, Rae." Rebecca half threw her arms up in defeat but caught herself before it threw off her balance on the bike. We spent the rest of the class in silence, but her comment about me taking the safe route lingered in my head for a while, biting the air with its harsh commentary.

It wasn't long before class ended—a little more than twenty minutes later, in fact—but it gave me enough time to start thinking about what I'd want to include on my list of risks to finally try. None of them included anything about Jake, but I was sure they'd be impressive and also require a lot of work on my part.

As soon as Kelly announced we were done and it was time to go into stretches, I hopped off my bike like it was on fire. It had as much to do with my glee of making it through the whole class as it did with me severely needing the relief in my legs.

"It should be against the law to do the things we

did to our butts and legs on a Saturday morning," I said, turning to Rebecca for the first time since my attempt at shutting down the Jake talk. I pulled a leg behind me, catching my foot with my hand, and felt the muscles in my body open up.

"Oh, my God, I know." Rebecca tried to catch her breath while she grabbed her right leg and crossed it in front of her left leg to mimic a seated position. "What the hell did we sign up for?" We both laughed again, any tension from earlier easily leaving us.

"Don't you kind of feel a little like Wonder Woman, too, though?" I asked, even surprising myself a bit. "It's amazing how a workout can be really hard, but as soon as you complete it, you feel like you can conquer the world."

"Maybe. Mostly, I feel like I can go home and take a nice long bath."

"Oooh," I exhaled. "Now, that sounds good, too."

We finished our stretches and began walking back to the front of the class, nervous about what Kelly might say to us as we passed her by.

"Bye, Kelly," we said in unison again.

"Bye!" It was clear she'd put on her best fake tone to get us out of her class as soon as possible.

"She probably hates us for how much we talked in her class," Rebecca giggled.

"Oh, yeah, I'm sure she couldn't wait for us to leave."

"Whatever, she'll be okay. More importantly, did

you think any more about the list while we were in there?"

"I did, actually," I said as we entered back into the locker room. "I came up with four potential risks so far."

"Oh, tell me! I'm waiting on pins and needles."

"All right," I said, using my fingers to mark the numbers as I went through them. "First is be more vulnerable when dating and risk falling in love again. Then, allow people to be there for me, you know, and not always feel like I'm the only one who has to be the strong friend or family member. Third, ironically, do fewer lists." I paused so we could both chuckle at that part and to give us a chance to key in our codes to get back into the lockers.

"Oh, yes, I can see this is going very well so far," Rebecca joked.

"I know," I said, nodding my head at how funny I sounded. "But I don't think I'll ever give up lists entirely. That's me. It's just giving myself more opportunities to be spontaneous and not as planned out with all my decisions."

"I like that. And the fourth?"

I let out a big sigh before listing the fourth item, nervous about even saying it aloud, but especially to Rebecca.

"Leave our comfy job for one where I have more control of what I say and where I can champion women who look like me more often."

"Rae…" Rebecca stopped herself and thought

about the best way she wanted to respond. I could almost see her pondering the different ideas in her head. Finally resolute, she continued, "I think that's one of the bravest things you could do. Honestly, they all are. But that one? I'm in awe!"

"You don't think I'm crazy? I mean, who thinks about leaving a job where her boss loves her and she's the author of the top article on the website at least once a week?"

"Someone who's not happy." Rebecca's matter-of-fact tone was not lost on me. "I don't think you're crazy at all. I love everything about this—oh! What if you rewarded yourself with a pair of shoes every time you finished something on the list?"

"Oh!" I was taken aback by the idea, but also kind of loved it. What could be more of a reward for someone like me than a brand-new pair of shoes as the ultimate checkmark? I wiped down my face and neck once more before grabbing my jacket from my locker. "I like that idea, Becs! It's sort of genius."

"And it won't just be the pleasure of buying new shoes," she interjected, agreeing. "They will also signify an investment, some intention behind your action. These are hard items, Rae. You're going to need some incentive to keep going with them."

"You're absolutely right," I said. This *was* going to be hard, but nothing spelled reward better than s-h-o-e-s. And I was essentially forcing myself to get four new pairs.

"Agh! Now that that's settled, what are you doing after this?"

"Umm, I don't know really. Probably get a salad down the street and then walk home. We're meeting up later to go see Christine this evening, but it's nice out today, and I could use the stroll. Wanna join?"

"Thanks, but no, thanks. Unlike you, who seems to enjoy being alone, I have a husband waiting on me to get back home."

I sighed. "You just won't let it die, huh?"

"Whaaat?" Rebecca smirked, knowing she'd accomplished her goal of putting the Jake idea back in my head. "You know it's all out of love, Rae. But you just remember. If you weren't so very single and wasting your time on all these stupid boys out here, you might have someone willing to rub that pained *tushion* of yours today." She emphasized her point by lightly smacking me on the butt right as she said *tushion*.

"Hey!" I screamed out. I was just about to remind her that doing a better job of being vulnerable was *on* the risk list, just not with people named Jake Saunders, when I realized she'd run out before I could turn around, effectively getting the last word that time.

Rude.

Alone again with my thoughts, I finished putting my jacket on—a slightly lined charcoal-and-turquoise windbreaker that was perfect for the unseasonably warm October weather—and walked toward the door. It was fifty degrees and sunny, and I wasn't going to let Rebecca, her grabby hands and her meddling push my buttons so much that I missed the beauty of the day.

Chapter Three

Once outside, I immediately breathed in the crisp, cool fall air, and then let out a sigh of relief. I'd made it through my first activity post "The Call," and it felt like a huge milestone had occurred.

Wow, DC can really be pretty when it wants to be, I thought, taking a look at the scenery around me. The brick sidewalks lined the streets of colorful row houses, tied together, but unique in their own ways, sometimes sporting two very contrasting hues, sometimes slightly blending into each other. A fountain to my left seemed to long for the days of summer when the children in the neighborhood would splash around in the water. Silent now, but still pretty, it made me yearn for springtime in the city when the trees that were losing their leaves would stand bright and green and towering in the sky, your ears filling with the sounds of laughter, and your nose delighting in the smells of empanadas and pastelitos on the street. To my right, towering over the other buildings in the neighborhood, also stood the expansive shopping mall, with my gym inside, to remind everyone of the sprawling growth that had happened in Columbia Heights within the past twenty years.

Yep, this was DC. Still packed with all the flavor and culture and traditions of the people who built it if you watched close enough, but also crawling with ambitious people ready to place more gyms and shopping malls on every corner they could.

I'd told Becs I would get a salad after I left the gym, but the truth was I didn't have much of an appetite. After a few steps in that direction, I changed my mind and decided to simply walk back home. Her statement about me not remembering the good times with Jake rang loudly in my ear and made me want time alone with my thoughts—just me and the city—more than food. I could remember the first time he broke my heart like it was yesterday, a fact that some of my friends didn't want to acknowledge. That pain still hurt and years later, was very fresh. He'd come running into my dorm room to tell me the great news: he was offered the investment banking job in New York, so come June, he was moving there. I was so excited for him. I'd been trying on my cap and gown when he barged in, but I ran into his arms right then and told him how proud I was of him and how I couldn't wait to see him take the world by storm. Jake had other plans, though. He kissed me and stepped back.

"I don't want a long-distance relationship, though, Rae."

"Oh." I was stunned and stumbled back a few paces as well.

"I'm sorry, I just don't think we could survive that. Not at twenty-one."

I could feel my heart crushing inside. Why had he come running to tell me this like it was good news?

"Then, what? Do you want me to move there, too?"

"No," Jake interrupted. "I... I think that would put too much pressure on us. Plus, you have a job offer here. I don't want you to give that up for me."

"Well, I wasn't saying..." I stopped myself once I realized what he was trying to say. "You don't want me anymore."

"Reagan, no, that's not what I mean." Jake put his hand on his forehead as he tried to find the words. "I—I don't know what I want, to be honest."

"I think it's pretty clear, actually."

I could play that conversation over and over in my head, word for word, each expression that we made, the way he walked out calmly before I crumbled into a ball of tears, the resolve I found within to never be that woman again, and the way I let myself get duped once more at Lance and Candice's wedding. Those memories were never too far away.

But despite all that, was Rebecca right? *Was I so focused on those two memories that I'd skewed everything under whatever is the opposite of rose-colored glasses? Do I owe him anything different?*

All these thoughts ran through my head as I continued walking home, the sun beaming from the sky and onto my skin. If you were looking from a window inside, you would have thought it was eighty or ninety degrees outside. Instead, the brisk air was getting chillier as I walked, almost acting like an opposite attraction force to the sun's rays. Or maybe it was like my relationship with Jake. You could almost lull yourself into believing it was perfect until you stepped outside and the wind reminded you of the truth. I zipped my jacket all the way up to my chin to help block out the cold. At least that had an easy enough fix.

"Watch out!"

It's April in DC, the weather is a perfect seventy with the sun shining bright, and we are lying out, basking in the sun on our college campus's yard. We are in our own world, despite the fact that everyone else obviously had the same idea to come outside and enjoy the day.

And while some are chillin' like us, many aren't lying around and laughing with their friends. They are practicing step routines, running from water gun fights, dancing to mixes of '90s R&B and hip-hop and playing some college version of hide-and-seek.

Some are even working on what seems to be the beginnings of a protest, one thing you could always
count on at Howard University. And of course, some
are playing football.

Which makes the football that has crashed into
our makeshift picnic, tossing the strawberries, cheese
and grapes onto our blankets and the ground, un-
surprising, but no less annoying.

"What the…" Robin screamed out. Jennifer has
grabbed the fried chicken in time to save a few pieces
of it, and Christine and I jumped out of the way before the ball hit one of us in the head, but we are none
too happy about the disruption. Gradually, we began
picking up our items and trying to put our arrangement back together. But we were so caught up, we
barely saw the cute, five-foot-eleven guy with the
body of a safety standing over us until he cleared
his throat.

"I'm so sorry, ladies," Jake said, extending out his
arm to help one of us up.

"What?" I asked, finally noticing him.

"I said I'm sorry," he repeated. "We didn't mean
for the ball to come this way. It's just that my boy
over there is the world's worst non-quarterback
ever. I keep telling him that thing is dangerous in
his hands."

Jake smiled, showing off the cutest dimple I'd ever
seen and pointed to his five friends, including one
who was shrugging in the background. I assumed
he was the culprit.

"Yeah, he shouldn't be allowed anywhere near a football or women." Robin, who'd finally noticed Jake as well, stared daggers back at him. She had no intentions of letting this guy think he could come and charm *the ladies*, as he'd called us. No, she wanted him to feel as uncomfortable as we did seeing a football come flying at our heads.

I, on the other hand, was already hooked and reached my hand toward his still outstretched arm, letting him help me stand up.

"Thank you," I mouthed to him, a smile starting to form on my face.

Jake held my hand in his and winked at me before returning to his back-and-forth with Robin. "Sounds like you could teach him a thing or two."

"I would destroy him and all your lil' homies, and then make you buy us new food to replace what you ruined."

Jake laughed. "For some reason, I believe you."

"You should," Christine chimed in. "My girl here is a football fanatic." She placed her arm around Robin's shoulder. *"Y tal vez un poco loca también,"* she joked.

"Whatever," Robin said, playfully removing her arm as if she was upset about Christine's crazy comment. "He at least owes us food."

"Fair, fair," Jake interjected. "We are happy to make up for this incident." I could feel his thumb tracing circles in my palm as he continued holding my hand, sending tidal waves of nerves throughout my body, all while he carried on a conversation with my girls as if he was doing nothing at all. Meanwhile, I was starting to have trouble standing. I had to do something quick before I collapsed in front of everyone.

"Umm, what's your name?" I asked, turning my body toward his.

"Jake."

"Okay, Jake, well, I'm Reagan, and this is Christine, Jennifer and Robin." I pointed to each of the girls as I introduced them, casually using my other hand to do so.

"Nice to meet you, ladies," Jake said to the group and then winked at me again. I think he could tell I was trying to defuse the situation and also maybe distract myself from the feels he was giving me as we stood there.

"What if…" I said, then paused. "What if we all went to lunch down the street at Oohs and Ahhs. On you guys."

"Done," he said without missing a beat. "I mean, if that's what the rest of you want?" He looked to the other girls with his best puppy-dog eyes, one by one, even wearing down Robin until she agreed.

"Great. Let me just tell my boys, and I'll be right back." He turned to me before leaving and leaned down so he could whisper in the corner of my ear. "To be clear, I don't want to let your hand go, but if I don't right now, I might never do it again." He took his other hand and slid it slowly across the line of my jaw until I slightly closed my eyes and let out an audible sigh. *Damn*, I thought as he went running back to his crew.

"What the hell was that?" Robin asked as soon as he was far enough away, bringing me back down to this world.

"I don't know!"

"Oh, *lo sé*," Christine joked. "I've seen this before. Reagan just creamed herself." She laughed uncontrollably.

"Oh, my God, Christine, that's disgusting. I did not."

"Mmm-hmm, well, something just happened," Robin said. "Because you basically just asked that man out on a date and used us all as bait."

"I just thought it would be a good way to make up for messing up our food. And you know Oohs and Ahhs has some of the best fried chicken in the city."

"Okay, she's not wrong about that," said Jennifer. "But just be careful, Rae. Dude seems like a charmer to the nth degree. He even had Robin eating out of his hands at the end."

We all laughed as we began picking up the blankets to fold them. Jennifer had already packed up whatever food hadn't been thrown in our plastic trash bag because it hit the ground. So we stood there waiting and watching as Jake explained the situation to his boys.

"Not a bad-looking specimen to be used by, though," Christine said, tilting her head to the side so she could get a full view of him from afar. "Mmm, mmm, mmm."

"Please," I said. "It won't even be like that. It's the end of our junior year. No one has time to be falling for someone or anything beyond just a little fun."

"Mmm-hmm," they replied in unison, with so much unbelief, it was almost hurtful.

Less than a few minutes later, we saw Jake walking back over to us, his friends in tow and his hand reaching for mine again.

"Y'all ready?" asked the quarterback.

"Nah, bruh, you owe us an apology first," Robin said. "I know y'all sent this one over here for a reason, but you're the one that needs to say the words." She folded her arms as she waited.

"You're right. I am very, very sorry," he said, bowing down in jest. "I promise it won't happen again."

"Uh-huh."

Jake laughed, and as he turned to me, I could finally understand part of why his smile was so perfect: he had the most beautiful, straight white teeth. The kind that made you think about licking them when you kissed. *He must have had braces as a kid.*

"Your girl's a bit of a hard-ass, huh?"

"She doesn't really believe in taking crap from anyone," I said, allowing his fingers to intertwine with mine.

"I can appreciate that. And what about you?"

"Me? I just tend to observe people for a while, see

if I can trust them. That helps me avoid being around a lot of people who might want to mistreat me."

"And do you think you can trust me?"

"I don't know yet. You seem hot like the sun, but that can be deceiving sometimes."

"How about this? I promise to always be honest with you, and you can observe me as long as you need to. I'll be here, because I want to know you." He raised our hands up to his lips, softly kissing mine without letting it go.

"Okay," I said, fully entranced by his brown eyes, and for the first time hoping my instincts were correct about someone thirty minutes into meeting them. "But first, let's get some soul food."

We looked up and noticed we were several paces behind the rest of the group who'd long ago left us to finish our conversation alone. Laughing, we ran to catch up with them, our hands still attached like it would hurt to break them apart.

The fifteen-minute walk back home felt like it took at least thirty-five minutes because my brain was on extreme overload. I could remember all the happy moments I wanted to, I realized, but that had been almost a decade ago. *What benefit did it serve me to remember the fond times when the most recent ones were hurtful?*

As I entered my place, I kicked off my sneakers and inhaled a long, deep, hard breath to try to release all the thoughts in my head. This was not the

Saturday I had in my mind when I woke up earlier that morning. But there I was, exhausted and needing a nap before we went back to see Christine later. I placed my keys on the hallway table, slipped off my jacket and hung it in the closet before taking another step. Maybe what I really needed to do was write, I wondered. That seemed to always clear my mind when I couldn't get out of my own head. Plus, I had a risk list to write down before I forgot what it included. Sighing once more, I made my way through my living room and into my bedroom.

I flicked on the light, walked past my white bed and tan end tables and straight to my shoe closet to find my shoe diary. Next to it was a set of six different color pens meant to symbolize how I felt at the time I wrote. Today was a blue pen day, for sure, for sadness, confusion, exhaustion and maybe a little bit of hope.

Chapter Four

It was a month and a half later before the doctors let Christine leave the hospital. In that time, she'd spent most of her days hooked up to machines checking her every breath, movement, heartbeat…for all I knew, maybe even her thoughts. The girls and I were there, not every day, but almost every day, reading to her and recounting funny stories. We'd made a pact that whatever we did, we wouldn't go in there and burden her with any of our current problems, especially as the weeks went by and it seemed like she'd never make it out of there.

We'd all started to really worry when she was still in there at Thanksgiving, but somewhere around the beginning of December, it felt like all her fighting spirit was beginning to pay off. I didn't know if it was her determination to not spend another holiday in the hospital or what, but by mid-December, they'd finally said the magical words: you can go home now, Ms. Vasquez.

You would have thought we'd each won an Olympic medal at the news, we were so excited to get our friend out of the cold prickliness of a hospital. Anyone who's ever spent any amount of time in one knows it is a place that doesn't allow for a lot of peace and quiet and tranquility, and Christine needed that more than ever. Her mom and boyfriend, Dominic, packed up her personal belongings so quickly it almost seemed like they were worried the doctors would come in and change their minds, but we understood why. As hard as being in a hospital was for the patient, it was just as difficult for the family, too.

A couple days had gone by since they released her when I walked up to Christine's familiar door, knocking on it to be let in. I'd wanted to give her some time with her family before the girls and I came by and started taking over, but it had taken everything in me to wait around for those two days to pass.

"Buenos dias," her mom said, dropping the "s" on both words and hugging me extra tight as I walked through the door. Mama Vasquez, like her daughter, was quite the lively character. She'd been born in the Dominican Republic, moved to the United States as a child and later to New Orleans when she decided to follow her dreams to become a chef. This all

meant she spoke and understood English perfectly, but when she was home or simply upset, she would automatically begin speaking in either her native Dominican dialect—which typically drops the "s" at the end of words—or a version that mixed Spanish and English, often toggling back and forth in the same sentence. It was how Christine developed her knack for dipping in and out of both languages and also how I learned just enough Spanish to understand them both when I needed to.

"Buenos días, Mama Vasquez." I stepped inside, removing my tan pea coat and slipping out of my ivory pointed-toe loafers as soon as I walked in. The familiarity hit me instantly. Her vintage lamp on the end table. Her collage of carnival masks flanking her sofa. The fireplace we'd all sat beside for so many years just having girl talk.

I couldn't believe it had been two months since I'd been in her apartment. I bit my tongue to stop the tears from welling up in my eyes.

"You can go straight to the back...*ella está esperando."*

"Gracias." I tiptoed my way to the back in case she'd fallen asleep before I got there and peeked in once I came upon her bedroom door. There she was, halfway perched up so the top of her body seemed like she was seated in a recliner, but the bottom half was relaxed in the bed.

"Mi amor? Hello." Christine's voice was tiny, but still raspy, as I stepped into her room. I could even

hear a hint of her boisterous tone trying to come out, peppered with the bit of Spanglish I'd heard many times over the years.

"Christine," I said, walking up to her and placing my hand on her right cheek. She was home, yes, but clearly still not out of the woods, mostly relegated to staying in her bed as her boyfriend and mom took turns bringing her food and water and to the bathroom when she needed.

"You look like you've been crying. *Cómo tú ta*?"

"Now you know I never cry," I replied, forcing a smile on my face. "I'm just happy to see you and hear your voice again." I sat down on the chair strategically placed next to her bed. I assumed it was the same chair her mom and boyfriend had taken turns sitting in for the past couple days. "Tell me, what are they saying in terms of recovery? How long do you now have to be in *this* bed?"

"They are still figuring everything out," Christine sighed. "I feel better for now, and my lungs are working again, so I'll probably be able to walk around for real in about another week. But I think I'm always going to have the complications that come with gastroparesis—the nausea, the feeding tubes, the constant worries I'll get another blood infection. It's exhausting, but it means I'm alive for now."

"Right," I said, suddenly at a loss for words. "That's… I mean, I didn't think I would ever hear your voice again without you sounding strained from all those machines." I leaned toward her, wanting to be as close as I could to my friend without suffocating her with my concern.

"Girl, I didn't think I would be able to do a lot of things. But I'm definitely blessed."

"You're a miracle, Chrissy," I blurted out.

"That's a lot of pressure, Rae." She could barely lift her head and there I was calling her a miracle. *What was I thinking?* I thought.

"No pressure! I'm just saying."

"One thing I've learned from this whole situation is that life is far too short. I knew it before, but this last bout in the hospital really brought it home for me."

"I think for me, too, honestly. I just kept replaying all the things we've ever done in my head, all the shenanigans we've been part of since high school, and I couldn't imagine..." I bit my tongue again, not wanting to cry and make her feel like she needed to comfort me. "I don't know. It just had me thinking a lot. I even started a risk list," I said, laughing. "I hadn't told you about it when you were in the hospital because I didn't want to bother you with it, but I think it's going to be good. You have said for a while that I've been living a—what was it you called it?"

"Vida cauteloso."

"Right. A cautious life."

"I like this," Christine said, straining to raise herself a little higher in the bed so she could talk easier. I jumped up to help, moving one of the pillows to her lower back to take off some of the pressure.

"Yes, this is very good." She paused. "Can I be honest? *Sabes que te quiero, pero* it hasn't been just a cautious life, *chica*."

"What do you mean?"

"This…fear of yours," she continued, "has also led you to even worse, *an amor cauteloso*—a cautious love."

"That's… Christine," I sighed, hesitating, and not finding the words to counter.

"It's not just you, though, *chica*. I was, too. It's how I can see it so clearly now. Something happened to you when things ended with you and Jake in college. It was like somewhere inside you decided you were better off, safer, if you stopped taking risks in everything. And don't get me wrong. That worked for a while. You have all the things every little girl grows up wanting, except love."

And happiness, too, I thought.

I sat back in my chair. For someone who could barely speak a month ago, Christine had just read me for filth. But I hadn't brought up the risk list so she could spend all our time trying to fix me; I wanted her to know how she was inspiring me. And also give her a chance to say whatever she needed about what she was going through without doctors and boyfriends and moms hovering in the background.

"So what are you going to do about your *vida cauteloso*?" I asked, changing the subject back to her. "Once you recover a bit, of course."

"You're not slick, but I'll give it to you this time."

She shifted in her bed again, trying to see if putting her weight on a different area of her body would help her regain some more comfort. "First thing's first, I'm going to focus my energy more on my singing and craft making. I'm realizing you can have all the money in the world, but you can't take it with you when you die. I'd just rather spend my time getting in all the experiences I can. And I'm going to work on spending more time with the people who positively impact my life."

"Wow."

"Sí. And it won't be easy. Especially because the doctors told me I will still have plenty of bad days, *pero mira,* I don't have the luxury of easy now. I need fulfilling. I need big rewards. I need to live the life I have as fully as possible."

"Who knew almost dying would make you such a guru," I joked. We both finally laughed, breaking the tension from all the sadness that had been in the air up to then.

"Por favor, you know I've been your Afro-Dominicana guru since we were fifteen. Remember that time you were making out with that guy—oh, what was his name?—when I drove you to his mom's salon and then had to scream out from the car for you to come up for air?"

"His name was Bobby. And how could I ever forget that? I was so embarrassed! All I heard was 'If you don't get your tail in this car, *mana,* we're going to leave you!'"

Christine couldn't stop laughing. "Yes, his name *was* Bobby! Oh, my God, that was hilarious. You two were just going to town like his mom couldn't come out of her salon at any moment and kick your curly-haired butt to kingdom come."

"I know," I laughed. "But he didn't care! And it made me not care." I put my head in my hands. Just saying it out loud helped me realize how foolish I sounded and probably looked back then, too.

"Exactamente. Y por eso me necesitas."

"Ha, that's true. I will always need you. Good thing you didn't leave me, huh?" I grabbed her hand and held on tight.

"You can't get rid of me that easily, *mana*. Plus, I would just haunt you anyway. You've got a risk list to finish."

A few hours later I checked my phone and noticed it was almost 8:00 p.m. We'd been laughing all day, but Christine's voice was starting to grow weaker and weaker as we continued.

"All right, lady," I said. "As much as I hate to leave you, I need to go to work in the morning, and you need your rest."

She didn't even put up a fight, but slightly closed her eyes and nodded. "You're right. I am starting to get pretty tired."

"I sort of figured as much, but just didn't want this to end," I replied, glancing up from my phone where I was inputting the address to my favorite salad place in my Uber app. My appetite was finally starting to come back to me, and I was craving one of their popular "donut salads"—a name Christine often used to describe the unhealthy salads on their menu.

"I'm not going anywhere, Rae. Don't worry."

"I think those are supposed to be my words to you," I said, getting up and kissing her on her forehead. I'd just received an alert that my ride was three minutes away, and I wanted to have time to say goodbye to her mom and boyfriend, put my loafers and coat back on and still get outside before I received the dreaded "your car will be leaving in two minutes" message. "Be good, okay?"

"Nunca," she joked, winking at me.

I walked back into Christine's living room, gathering my coat and kissing Mama Vasquez and Dominic goodbye in one swoop. "Thank you all for letting me come see her."

"Reagan, you are welcome here anytime," her mom replied. "Honestly, if it were up to her, you girls would probably be here every day."

"It won't be every day, but I promise you might get tired of us as much as we are here."

"No, the smile you put on my baby's face will be worth it every single time."

"Thanks, Ma," I said, giving her one more kiss.

"Gracias, querida."

I stepped out into the cold air just as a silver Honda with flashing lights pulled up. "You're Reagan?"

"Yes, I am," I said, climbing into the backseat on the right side.

"You're going to Chopt, right?"

"Yes, definitely," I sighed and picked up my phone again. There was only one voice I wanted to hear after being with Christine all day, and it wasn't the Uber driver's. I scrolled to "Mom" in my phone and waited for her to answer.

"Hey, baby." Her voice sounded like that of an angel.

"Hey, Mom, got a minute?"

Chapter Five

"*Cher*, you know I always have time for my first-born. What's up, Rae?"

I chuckled to myself; if it was one thing my mom loved calling me, it was her firstborn. There were times I thought it was a dig at my grandparents because she'd grown up as their first kid and had to bear the brunt of helping them take care of the other six children that came after her. Other times, I thought she was trying to be relatable in my mom's own way, which for her always sort of seemed to come off a little passive-aggressive.

In fact, Maria Chevalier Doucet, pronounced Mah-ree-ahh, was known for the kind of advice that started with "Well, if I were you, *cher*, I would…" It was endearing at times, because she was the kind of person who walked into a room and forced you to adore her since she stole your attention at "hi"; but also often annoying because it usually preceded advice she wanted to give especially if she knew you didn't want to hear it. And that was the paradox of my mom—she was a force to be reckoned with, a sixty-year-old Louisiana Creole diva mother of four who knew how to make you love her even if she annoyed you. I was willing to risk all that for the comfort of her voice.

"I'm leaving Christine's now," I said, leaning back into my seat.

"Oh, yes, how is she?"

"You know Christine. Always worried about everyone else when she's the one who just got out of the hospital and still has at least two more weeks before she can move around freely."

"Wow, you mean you're best friends with someone who acts just like you and thinks about others more than herself? That's just so odd." Her sarcasm sliced through the phone, and I could almost hear her giggling to herself for how perfectly she played that part of our conversation.

"I called because I needed you to help me relax after a whole day of being strong for Chrissy, Mom, not for a lecture."

"What? I would never give you a lecture, Rae." It was utterly amazing how she could put on such a shocked expression over the phone, especially when she was literally doing the thing that I'd called her out on. "I just…you know, if I were you, I'd think about how I feel the need to be strong all the time. I know you've been hurt more than any of us even know, baby, but you hold it all in. I bet right now, you're in a car, and your shoulders are higher than the Empire State Building."

I took a deep breath while listening to her and noticed my shoulders were tight and scrunched up toward my ears. She may have been correct about that part, I guessed. But still, this wasn't the calming talk I'd been hoping for. Even though I'd had a great time laughing with Christine, it was mentally exhausting pretending I wasn't scared for her life every second of every day. Rolling them down, I tried to restart the conversation. "Mom, thank you for your concern. Truly. But I really just wanted to hear you say everything is going to be okay."

"Ohhhh, of course everything is going to be okay, *cher*," she said, quickly reminding me of my mom's frustrating duality. "But I'm your mom. I want you to be *more* than okay."

"I know, Mom," I sighed. "I'm trying."

As we drove through the neighborhoods, I saw a few snowbanks left over from the last storm, still lingering on the edge of the sidewalk, the white now darkened by the steps of those walking on it daily. I'd have to be careful stepping back out of my ride to make sure I didn't go sliding down the street. Loafers were cute for wearing to someone's house, but not exactly sensible once I decided to make the detour to Chopt before heading home. Regardless, I was just looking forward to my favorite salad at this point—romaine lettuce, panko chicken, pecorino cheese, tomatoes, cucumbers and eggs, with Caesar dressing. Especially since my mom hadn't exactly provided the comfort that I was seeking.

We pulled up to the restaurant, and I carefully lifted my feet out of the car, one loafer at a time. "Mom, I'm going to have to call you back," I said. "I'm going in now, and you know I don't like to be on the phone when I'm ordering."

"I know, baby. Call me back later."

"Will do. Love you."

"I love you, too."

I knew she meant it, but boy, that call had gone the exact opposite of how I'd wanted. No less anxious, now I was just really hungry on top of everything. I hung up the phone and took my place in line, dutifully staring at the menu on the wall like a bad habit since I already knew what I wanted. There were three other people in front of me, so I guess I didn't exactly have to rush my mom off the phone. But better to be safe than sorry with Maria; who knows where that call could have gone if it had been five minutes longer?

While waiting, I noticed the door open and saw a young guy come in, dreadlocks down his back, with a hoodie peeking out of his winter coat. With him was a little bouncing baby girl in her stroller, filling the quiet space with her baby coos. *What a nice image*, I thought. A present father out taking a stroll with his daughter at night. It was only after I stared closer that complete dread came over my whole body. This was no regular young guy with a kid; it was my college ex-boyfriend who I broke up with two months before meeting Jake. If Jake was the one who set fire to my heart and ripped it apart, Matthew had been the one to light the first flame. He'd convinced me we were the best of friends for two years, then that us dating was the only natural progression, and then finally, that you couldn't even trust your best friend not to cheat on you.

Maybe he wouldn't see me, I hoped. Or at least have the courtesy to pretend like he didn't. I placed my order and tried positioning myself away from him while the guy behind the counter mixed all my ingredients together. It didn't take long before I heard his voice, loud and clear, calling my name. *So much for that.*

"Reagan, wow. Is it really you?" Matthew was still only feet away from the entrance, so to get my attention, he practically screamed my name across the whole restaurant. To say I was embarrassed was an understatement.

"Hi, Matthew," I said, turning toward him and trying to plaster a smile on my face.

"How are you?" He didn't bother to wait until he was next to me to start talking, but instead walked and pushed that damn stroller, even as he began asking me questions.

"I'm good. Just picking up a salad to go." I reached behind me to get my bowl from the server and tapped my phone on the scanner to pay for the meal, hoping that he would take the "to go" hint and leave me alone.

"Well, obviously, Reagan. I'm not blind," he responded as he finally stood directly in front of me. At five foot eight, Matthew wasn't especially tall, but he still managed to position himself where it seemed like he was towering over me.

"Still sarcastic as ever, huh, Matthew?"

"I'm still me," he said, grinning smugly.

Right. How did I ever fall for this guy again?

"But other than getting a salad, what's going on with you?"

"Matthew, I—"

"Listen, I know we didn't end well, Rae. I'm just hoping everything's all right with you these days," he said, interrupting me before I could go on my spiel about how I wasn't sure why he thought it was necessary for us to have this conversation.

So much for me finishing that thought, I guess.

"I heard about Christine being really sick, and I know how close you two were. I'm assuming you still are?"

"We still are, yes," I said, slightly calming myself down, but still ready to get out of this impromptu meeting as fast as I could. "She's doing better now. Out of the hospital. And I'm good." I kept my responses short and sweet. It wasn't like I wanted to sit down and catch up with him over donut salads, after all.

"Not married yet, though, right?"

"What?" I hadn't expected that question or that turn in the conversation.

"I just noticed you're not wearing a ring."

"Oh." I looked down at my bare left ring finger like it had betrayed me. "No, I'm not married. I see you are, though. And with a kid!" I gestured to the little girl who'd since fallen asleep in the stroller next to us.

"Yeah, I am. And two kids actually."

"Oh, wow. Okay," I said, suddenly stunned. This day had surely been a roller coaster of emotions for me, and it was apparently only getting worse. "Congratulations then, Matthew. I'm happy for you." I clenched my jaw, trying to get the last part of that statement out with a hint of bitterness sliding out of my mouth.

"Thanks," he continued. "I'm kind of surprised you're not married, though. Just knew you would beat me to the altar."

"Ha," I chuckled nervously. "As luck would have it, I did not." *Yep, it was definitely time for me to get out of there before I ended up saying something I would regret.*

"That's right. I forgot I heard you took the career woman route. You're this big-shot writer now, yes? I've heard a lot of people say you're doing some great stuff around politics."

"You could maybe say that," I replied, my plastered smile turning to a cringe. Was he trying to torture me for doing the smart thing and breaking up with his funky self when I found out he cheated on me? It sure seemed like it. "I mean, yeah, I am…just also thinking of making some changes lately."

"Oh, okay." His pause was deafening. "I'm sure you'll turn things around soon, then."

I wanted to punch him in his face right in front of his child and in front of everyone in the restaurant. What was that? Pity? No one had said anything about needing to turn my life around.

I steadied my breathing before responding. "There's no need to turn things around. As I said before, I'm doing all right. Things are good." I paused once more for dramatic effect. "But if you don't mind, I do have somewhere to be, so I must get going."

He didn't have to know that my somewhere was my living room couch in front of my TV while I plowed my salad into my mouth. I turned away from him and began walking toward the door in my best attempt possible to stop from screaming: "Are you kidding me? You were probably the first person to ruin my idea of men and relationships! *You* put me on this path that you now think needs to be turned around. And now you want to pity me? Ugh!"

But Matthew wasn't interested in ending the conversation. He kicked the lock off the stroller and followed behind me.

"No problem, Rae. I get it, and I hope I didn't offend you. It's just... I really have heard great things. Figured you were living the perfect life by now."

"There's no such thing as a perfect life, Matthew. It's just what you make of the one you've got. Christine has taught me that." In the glass doors of the restaurant, I caught my reflection and noticed my loafers again, standing out among the mostly tan-and-green interior. It gave me the sense of confidence I'd lacked throughout most of our conversation. I straightened and turned back toward him. "One other thing. I'd prefer you not call me Rae anymore, okay? That's what my friends call me. And we're not friends."

"Reagan!" Now it was his chance to be stunned. "How can you say that? There was a time when we were best friends."

"There was a time when I *thought* you were my best friend," I said, my voice rising with anger, so high that I could see people stopping to pay attention to us out of the corner of my eye. "And then one of the hardest days happened to me, and my actual best friends came to my dorm and helped put me back together. How ironic you asked about Christine when she, Robin and Jennifer were literally the ones who came racing to my dorm room when that girl called me to say she'd been seeing you for months."

"Reagan, I don't think we need to go down this road again."

"Oh, we don't?" I asked, flabbergasted. "You don't

get to decide that, Matthew. You don't get to decide how I remember you." I stood even taller and placed my salad on a tabletop next to me so I could fully express myself without worrying that I would drop it on the floor. I knew with how loudly I was speaking to him that I was making a scene at this point and just didn't care. "What I remember, and what I will always remember, is that one month after losing my virginity with you, my friends stood over me and watched the tears pour from my eyes and blanket the brown suede material of my Birkenstocks. It was Robin, of all people, who stopped Christine from coming after you that night. She wanted to bang on your door and unleash holy hell for hurting me like you did. And it was Jennifer who held me until my shoulders stopped shaking. So I will go down that road as much as I want to, and I will tell you what you can and can't call me!"

I made a point to look him in the eyes so he knew I was serious and then turned around on the heels of my loafers, grabbed my salad and trotted out of there as fast as I could.

In my head, he was standing there, mouth agape, trying to figure out what had just happened. And that made me happy. Petty. But happy nonetheless.

I climbed into my next Uber ride—which thankfully came only one minute after I called it—and settled into my seat. Ten more minutes and I'd be back in the comfort of my apartment, away from

ex-boyfriends who cluelessly brought out the worst
in me, reminders from my mom about how great the
outside world thought my job was and the pressure
of being the perfect friend for Chrissy when all I really wanted to do was scream and shout about how
unfair it was that *my* best friend was the one suf-
fering from a chronic illness. I leaned back farther
into my seat and thought more about why I despised
crying so much. It had almost sickened my stomach
admitting to Matthew how much I'd cried the night
I found out about his affair. *But wasn't that natural?*
Didn't he probably assume I'd cried?

He never saw it, though. I didn't flinch a bit when
we argued during our breakup, no matter the numer-
ous hurtful things he said to me, like how I was good
enough as a girlfriend until he'd pledged and become
the man on campus or how he was open to me being
one of his girls if I wanted. I'd learned early on that
crying was a form of weakness, so he may not have
known it at the time, but he was never going to get
that out of me again.

In fact, if I really thought about it, I couldn't
remember a time when tears weren't shameful or
meant to be hidden. And my examples of this fact
were plenty: my dad struggling to withhold his tears
when his mom died; my grandfather sneaking away
from the family to cry when my uncle died; my mom
trying to hold her head up and remain strong when
my dad left. Even the refrains from family members
when the children would act up signified that cry-

ing was inherently wrong. "Don't make me give you something to cry about," they'd say, as if that was the worst thing in the world, even if it was an empty threat. And inevitably the children would quickly straighten up and stop whimpering. They'd stop expressing their pain.

As far as I was concerned, the strongest people I knew in this world were made weak through their tears flowing, and that wouldn't be me. Not in front of Matthew or Jake, and after that night, not even my friends. That was the last time any of them saw me break down crying beyond a tiny tear or two for a *Grey's Anatomy* episode or Mufasa dying in *The Lion King*.

It wasn't that I didn't cry; it was that I didn't let others see it. But maybe it was time to change that a little bit. Stepping out of my Uber, I walked up to my apartment building and gingerly took the steps to the front door, making sure not to slip on the wet ground. It was too late tonight, but I vowed to call Robin and Jennifer for a long-overdue girls' night in just as soon as I had some time to myself to process it all.

Chapter Six

"You mean to tell me you ran into Matthew, of all people, and you didn't send out the bat signal for backup immediately?"

Sitting in my living room three days later, Robin and Jennifer listened intently as I recounted with a mouth full of nachos how crazy Sunday had been. And most of it was perfectly normal and familiar until I got to the part about running into Matthew while picking up dinner; that was when they each perked up in their respective places—Robin sitting up straight while on my couch and Jennifer moving from a seated position on the floor to one on her knees. Robin was also none too pleased about hearing of the meeting for the first time days later.

"It wasn't like I wanted to stay there any longer than I needed to, Rob! C'mon." I picked up another nacho filled with black beans, shredded cheese, steak, pico de gallo and jalapeños. There was a time when we had Nacho Thursdays once a week, but that had petered out with an influx of happy hours, dates and unexpected long hours at work—from us all. Sunday's events were the perfect excuse for me to ask the girls if we could reinstate our tradition.

"I know, but I just can't believe that fool tried you like he did. The nerve!"

"Don't worry. I told him that even fun-loving Christine wanted to kill him that night in college."

"I did, too," interjected Jennifer. "But you were so devastated. I had to focus on that first."

"I know, honey... Never again, though, right?" I raised my margarita glass in the air for Robin and Jennifer to join me for an impromptu toast.

"Tuh, ain't that the truth," Robin agreed, her "lob" flipping on its own with her excitement.

We clanked our glasses together and took sips of our drinks before continuing.

"Oh, my God," Robin said as she put down her glass. "I can remember that night like it was yesterday. All I heard was you crying and Christine muttering, 'I'll kill him' under her breath and racing to the door, her long, thick black hair giving her some sort of magic-like speedy powers. I really thought she was going to do it, too. It was nuts!"

"I remember jumping up when it didn't seem like you could hold her back, and my Birkenstocks flying off my feet and into the air," I laughed.

"Yes, that's right! They flew off your feet, didn't they?" Jennifer asked rhetorically.

"Yes, yes, they did."

"Serves you good for still wearing those old-ass shoes from high school. Why did you still have those?" asked Robin.

"Okay, that's rude. They were my comfort shoes."

"Comfort shoes," Jennifer scoffed, trying desperately to hold in her giggles. "I mean, what Black girl even wears Birkenstocks?"

"Don't do me like that! You know I didn't go to a majority Black school in high school."

"That's true, all right. I won't joke on you too bad. I don't think they did a very good job, though."

"No, they definitely did not." I took another sip of my margarita and glanced down at the tan, fluffy hamster slippers I was wearing, hoping they wouldn't get joked on, too. To help, I turned the conversation back to Robin. "But to be fair, I hadn't planned on trying to stop a fight from happening that night."

"To be fair, I was all of a hundred and thirty-five pounds soaking wet in college, so I don't know why I thought I could stop anyone from leaving that room," Robin said. "We were all a little smaller then, but my grown woman thighs didn't come in until about two years after we graduated. Now, thankfully…" She slapped her legs and sang the rest of her statement to the tune of City High's "Caramel": "I'm five-nine with thick thiiiiighs."

"Lord, help us." Jennifer rolled her eyes and grabbed a nacho, stuffing it into her mouth so she wouldn't say anything else about Robin's singing or her thick thighs. "Can we talk about something serious now?"

Robin and I both groaned. "Sure," we said in unison.

"I've been so excited about having a serious conversation over nachos and margs all day, Jenn. You didn't know?" I winked at her and slumped down in my chaise a bit, hoping my sarcasm hadn't gone too far. I hadn't quite mastered my mom's endearing way of using it yet.

"Well, whether you were looking forward to it or not, we're having it. This is what friends do."

I slumped farther down into my chair, feeling like a kid who'd just been chastised by her sweet-as-pie big sister.

"Okay, okay. Just please spit out whatever it is you want to say. The suspense is making it worse!"

"I agree," Robin said in the distance as she poured herself another margarita from the pitcher. She had the right idea. I probably should get another drink before hearing whatever Jenn wanted to say but was hesitating to. I leaned back up and motioned to Robin to pass me the pitcher as well. Pouring my glass, I finally heard Robin say the magic words: "I want to talk about your list."

"*My* list?" I asked.

"No one else has one, Rae," Robin added. I was pretty sure she was just finding out while I was that this was what Jenn wanted to discuss and wanted to make sure the heat stayed on me and didn't come her way. She wasn't slick.

"Okay. What about it?"

"Have you done anything with it yet?"

"What's your definition of *done*?" I gulped down my latest glass of margarita, hoping to give myself a little more time to answer my newfound interrogation.

"This isn't Never Have I Ever. We're not giving definitions to try to find loopholes here. *You know* what I mean… Robin, help me out here."

"It has been two months since you told us about it, Rae." Robin knew she was being such a traitor in that moment, so she poured herself another glass, too. This was the problem with Jenn's super-sweet demeanor and her "wear your heart on your sleeves" personality; it meant when she wanted to assert herself, no one felt like they could tell her no.

I peered at her sheepishly as she casually fixed her pixie cut despite not having a mirror, all while waiting for me to respond. Instinctively, I also put my hands to my hair and began twirling around one of my loose curls. "I wrote it down," I finally offered.

"Mmm-hmm." Jennifer didn't even look up and I could tell that wasn't enough. And Robin was still stuffing her face with nachos, so she was not going to be any help bailing me out of this one.

"Here's the thing. No, not really. But it's not like I've had a ton of time to do so since then. Peter has been up my ass about more stories since that last one was a big hit. We're all focused on Christine. I

had the Matthew sighting. I've started spinning...
you know, it's a lot."

I was hoping my attempt to tug at Jennifer's heart-
strings would help me a bit. It wasn't like she was
mad at me, after all; this was just her trying to show
tough love—something she did maybe once a year,
and it was clearly my turn this year. Last year Robin
was the one caught in the fire because she'd mentioned wanting to try therapy to Jennifer and hadn't
seen anyone six months later. *That was absolutely
why she was staying as far as she could from the
conversation.*

"I get that. And those would be legit reasons if
only some of them couldn't be solved by actually,
you know, doing. Something. On. The. List." She
spaced out her words for dramatic effect and it was
almost like those memes where you see the Black
woman clapping emojis in between each word, except it was in real life. She was "Black woman-
clapping emoji-ing" me with her words.

"You're right. I know."

"Thing is, Rae," Robin interjected. "Jennifer is
probably being unnecessarily a hard-ass right now,
but she's not wrong. If you say you want to take more
risks because you're not happy, you're emotionally
drained, you feel like you've been checking off all
the boxes of what you should do instead of finding
out who you are...that's not something life is going
to just miraculously help you make time for. You've
got to just do it."

Fine time for her to stop stuffing her face with

nachos now, I thought. But I heard them both loud and clear; it was time for me to stop saying I was going to do something with the list and actually set about trying one of them. Especially since I'd also told Christine over the weekend. It was only a matter of time before she was joining in with them to gang up on me, and I did not want that.

"You're both right," I relented. "So what now?"

"Now you tell us which of the four has been on your heart the most. Which one do you want to try to tackle first?" Jennifer asked.

I sat there silent for a second, and even closed my eyes, trying to figure out which one made the most sense to work on first. None of them would be easy so it wasn't like I could pick the lowest-hanging fruit and start there, and each of them was going to require a ton of work before I felt comfortable checking off that I'd completed it. It's not like I could just go on one date and say, yes, I checked off that whole "being vulnerable and open to falling in love again" thing. Next!

There was one that was the most tangible, however. And it was the same one that was probably going to shake up the perception of my perfect life the most from the people who didn't really know me. I opened my eyes and saw Robin and Jennifer both sitting down and waiting for me, the support they always were, and it gave me the courage to finally say it.

"The job," I half whispered. Clearing my throat, I tried again. "The job," I repeated. "As scary as it's going to be, I can't keep doing stories that don't reflect me and what I'm passionate about."

"Rae, I'm proud of you," said Jennifer, rising up from the floor to come closer to me. She put her arms around me and whispered, "You got this. I know you do."

"Yeah," I responded. She let her arms down and sat next to me on the chaise. "I don't even know where to start with it, though. I haven't looked for a new job in years."

"Oh, that's the easy part," Robin said, reaching for the pitcher to pour us all a fresh round of margaritas. "The hard part, besides this conversation, is going to be letting your old job go when you find the new one. Just because, you know, comfort."

"That's true," I said. "As much as Peter frustrates me sometimes, at least it's the devil I know. And plus, I have Becs there, too."

"But Rebecca is one of us now. She's not going anywhere," Jennifer said. "And Peter will be okay. *This* is about Reagan now, and I'm so excited for what you end up taking on."

"And, we'll both be here to help you job search, too."

"Are y'all also going to help me search for the shoes that I buy when I complete the risk?"

"Uhhhh, that's a given," Robin replied. "In fact, that's really what we should be doing now instead of all this mushy crap. Go get your laptop, so we can pull up some of the sites you go on to get your sample sale designer shoes."

"Oooh, yes, I'm going to enjoy this part so much more than having to be the stern friend."

"Literally, no one told you that you needed to go all hard-ass Jennifer, so you get no sympathy, friend." I swished back to my bedroom in my comfy slippers and picked up my laptop to bring it back to the living room. In the distance, I spied them high-fiving each other on a job well-done. *Nothing like having persistent best friends, that was for sure.*

"I actually have a pair I've kind of had my eye on," I shouted as I made my way back to the living room.

"Of course you do. That would be the part of the list you've been working on instead of the risk part. 'What else can I add to my shoe closet?'" Jennifer replied, snickering.

"Okay, do you want to see the shoes or keep playing my life tonight?"

"You *know* we want to see the shoes. Stop making us wait."

"Okay," I replied with glee, plopping back down in my chaise. I opened up the laptop and went to my bookmarks, landing on the page I'd saved just a couple weeks before. "Feast your eyes on these beauties, ladies. Aren't they just to die for?"

Part 2: Trying on All the Wrong Shoes

"…it's not so much about the shoes, but the person wearing them."

—Adriana Trigiani, *Viola in Reel Life*

Chapter Seven

This isn't going to be so bad, I thought, listening to the familiar sound of my heels *click-clacking* on the linoleum floor as I stepped off the elevator at my job. It's not like I was leaving my job today; just telling Becs it was coming. I'd finally started job searching. So why was I so nervous?

I glanced down at my shoes and wiped my sweaty hands down the sides of my thighs, along the seams of my mustard-yellow tapered pants that cut off just above my ankles. Paired with my ankle-strapped, pointed-toe silver stilettos and my cream blazer, it probably appeared as if I was dressed more appropriately for the spring than a few days before Christmas. But I needed to wear something light on what could very well be the first of my last days in the office.

Walking down the long and deserted hallway that led to my and Rebecca's desks, I was once again grateful that we'd likely have the next hour to ourselves. It would give me just enough time to catch her up on Nacho Thursday and see if we were going to do anything over the weekend. I was steps away from her desk before I realized she wasn't there.

Oh, that's odd. She was always there or would have texted me to say she wasn't coming. I checked my phone to see if maybe I'd missed a message, but no. It wasn't until I fully walked up to her desk that I saw her trench coat was casually draped over her chair and her laptop open. *Oh, okay, so she was in the office somewhere.*

Selfishly, I wondered where she was at a time when I needed to give her such big news but sat down at my desk anyway, opened my laptop and began checking my emails. Oooh, responses from Brittney Cooper and Kimberlé Crenshaw. Maybe today was going to be better than I even expected. If I could get either of them to speak to me about the topic of intersectionality, maybe I could finally get Peter to okay my pitch.

"Hey, Rae." I heard Becs calling my name as she walked up. She sounded groggy, but also a little excited.

"Hey, where were you? And why do you sound tired?"

"I had to be here even earlier than normal this morning. You didn't see the email from Peter? They needed IT to come in to do some backups to the site. Sounds like we got another investor and they're asking to see more traffic. The higher-ups wanted to make sure our site could handle it."

"Oh. Okay." I scrolled through my emails again and saw the one she was referring to. *I guess I missed it with my excitement over the other two.*

"Plus, I got a promotion this morning."

"What? OMG, Becs, congratulations!" I jumped up from my desk to hug her and held on tight for about ten seconds. "I'm so happy for you—wait, does that mean Peter is here at nine in the morning?" I glanced at my watch to make sure I wasn't delusional about the time.

"You really did not read that email," she said, chuckling.

"I did not. But it sounds like I should have." I scrunched up my face as I bounced back to my desk. Who knew I'd miss so much since leaving yesterday evening?

I quickly clicked on Peter's name and saw his message:

Team, I'll be in early tomorrow morning. We have some B.I.G. developments happening with some B.I.G. investors. Rebecca and Tatum, we're going to need all IT folks on hand tomorrow, so I'm hoping you'll be available to pitch in as needed.

Leave it to Peter to say so little in something that was supposed to be a heads-up to his employees. I turned back to Rebecca, incredulous. "This email? This is the one you've been harping on me to read? The one that said absolutely nothing?"

"Well, you would have known he was here early."

"Which for Peter could mean ten-thirty. I can't believe you. Is this 'promotion Becs' speaking?"

"Oh, please." She threw her scarf in my direction in protest, but I caught it midair. "You know, I will forever be your big sister and call you out on your crap. It doesn't take a promotion for me to do that."

"This I know." I rolled my eyes, leaned back toward her and lowered my voice to a whisper. "And good thing because I also have news for you. I finally started job searching last night." With Peter already in, I made sure to keep my statement short and sweet. There was no use in getting fired before I'd found a new job.

"Rae, that's great news! I've been wondering but didn't want to push."

"Don't worry. Jenn and Robin did that for you. They pulled good cop-bad cop on me last night."

"Good for them!"

"Only problem was when we actually started checking out some of the job listings, they were a mess. One was for a technical writer, but they wanted you to have at least six years' experience in reporting and in simplifying technical/legal language, a law degree and were only offering fifty-six thousand dollars."

"A year?"

"Mmm-hmm. Amazingly, that wasn't the worst one. No, that honor goes to the listing for cat writers for a pets' blog that specified you must love cats over dogs, be willing to write various topics on cats four times a week and edit the writing of other cat writers. Serious inquiries only, of course."

"That can't be real."

"Oh, but it was," I snorted. "Thank God it was just the first night, but I'm definitely going to make sure I narrow my choices down a little better next time. And probably not drink tequila while searching."

Rebecca could barely contain her giggles. "That sounds like a good plan."

"What sounds like a good plan?" The two of us were so in our own world, we hadn't noticed when Peter snuck up on us, catching the tail end of Rebecca's joke.

"Oh, nothing," I said, rolling my chair back to my desk. "Just girl talk, Peter. Nothing to concern yourself with."

"Is this what you all do this early in the morning? Just tell jokes at your desks?"

"One may never know. Unless—" Rebecca gasped "—you plan on showing up before 10:00 a.m. regularly now."

"No, I hate being here this early. You never have to worry about this being something I do very often."

Rebecca and I giggled quietly at our desks. We knew Peter was serious about his hatred for what he called "being at work early," but only in enter-

tainment industries was 9:00 a.m. considered early.
Peter had no idea how lucky he was. Rebecca and I
had both endured the 7:00 a.m. expectations of the
corporate world for short periods of time when we
were younger, so this was a luxury. But he was the
boss; it wasn't like we were going to be the ones to
bust his bubble.

Peter barely registered our giggles at his expense.
"Reagan, can you join me in my office? There's
something I wanted to talk to you about."

"Sure," I replied, looking to Rebecca for some
clue on what he wanted. She shrugged her shoulders,
just as confused as I was.

Click-clacking back down the hallway to Peter's
office felt a little like being walked to the principal's
office. Sure, it didn't necessarily mean you were in
trouble, but it felt like it did. And just my luck, other
supervisors must have warned their employees they
would be in the office early, too, because I saw more
faces watching me than ever at this time of the morning. *Great, everyone will be here just in case I get
fired.* Suddenly, my silver stilettos didn't seem like
the right pick for the day, after all.

"I really just wanted to take a moment to tell you
how much your work has improved lately," Peter
said, easing my nerves as we stepped into his office.
"I'm really excited about where you're going with
your articles these days. It's no longer just the same
rigmarole about Beltway politics and speculations."

He closed the door behind me and gestured to me to sit down in one of his chairs.

"Oh! Thank you, Peter."

"That said, I want you to commit to even more. And to do that, I want to offer you that promotion you've been angling for. We know you've got *it*, Reagan, so no more holding back."

"Really?" I was stunned. Peter was saying everything I'd wanted to hear him say for the past two years, but of course, it was coming the day after I'd decided to start searching for another job. Now what would I do? I needed more information, that was for sure. "Does this mean I can do more stories championing women, dig into our complex needs and really tackle some of the issues beyond what happens because of the White House?"

"It means you won't even have to ask. I'm offering you an editor position where you'll run your own vertical. I'll still have some say-so in your content, but this will be your baby."

"Oh, my God." I had no idea what to say in that moment. My legs went numb under me, my fingers felt tingly and my mouth could barely move. I'm sure I seemed like I was out of my mind sitting across from him, but I was using all of my energy to formulate words, so I didn't have it in me to also change the look on my face.

"I'm guessing that's a yes, you accept."

"I… Well, I need to think about it," I blurted out. "Is that okay? Can I think about it?"

"Of course."

"Okay, that's what I'm going to do, then." I gathered myself well enough to stand up out of Peter's chair and began walking to his door. My hand on the knob, I turned back around to see if I could tell what he was thinking. I was usually pretty good at observing people, especially Peter, but this one caught me off guard. I wasn't sure if it was because I'd come in so resolute that I'd be leaving in the New Year, or what. But I'd missed all the signs—and there were plenty. Big investor. Supervisors in early. Becs getting a promotion, too. Why hadn't I realized this was where this was going? Maybe it was because I wasn't sure how I'd be able to turn it down. "Thanks for the offer, Peter. I appreciate it."

"You earned it, Reagan. Now, go keep proving me right that you deserve it."

I walked out of his office, completely unsure of my path going forward, but knowing I needed to find the leg movement to get back to my desk before people started asking me questions. Less than thirty minutes earlier, I'd been so confident, so certain I was doing the best thing by taking the risk of leaving my job of four years that no longer made me happy, but this was a different job, too, just at the same company. *Was the promotion a sign I should stay?*

If anyone could help me talk through something this monumental, it was Christine. But I wanted her focus to be solely on her recovery right now, not me. Rebecca, Robin and Jennifer were normally great listeners, too, but on this topic, they were already invested in wanting me to leave. I worried about their impartiality. But who else? Certainly not my mom.

And then it hit me. The person I would have wanted to talk to the most was Jake. There was a time when he could help me calm down all the thoughts swirling in my head and figure out which one to listen to; which thought wasn't being driven by fear or expectations, but was just the thing I wanted. A very big part of me craved that kind of reassurance, but another part just as equally big hated that I thought of him in that moment. That flood of emotions came pouring to the surface—the hurt of missing someone, the shame of missing that particular someone and the frustration of having not controlled those feelings better—as I made it back to Rebecca's desk.

"So what did he want?"

"To offer me my own vertical on the website."

"Whoa. That's big, Rae."

"I know." I ran my fingers through my hair and plopped down into my chair. "I asked him to give me time to think about it."

"Okay, that's good. No need to say yes or no at this very second."

"Exactly. But now I have too many things running through my head…do you have plans tonight?"

"Not really. Oliver wants to celebrate my promotion this weekend but he's working late tonight, so we can save that for tomorrow. Why, what were you thinking?"

"I'm thinking we need to get out—all of us. You, me, Robin and Jenn. We'll celebrate your promotion and my offer and most importantly, drink away all the cares of the world," I said, grabbing Rebecca's hands to pull her out of her seat and give her a quick twirl.

"Done, silly bird. Count me in. Just let me text my husband and let him know I'll be home late."

"Good. And I'll text the girls. It's about time we put our creaky knees to the test again."

Later that night the four of us strutted up to the entrance of one of DC's premier nightclubs, looking and feeling like a cross between your favorite girls' group from the 1990s and four of the "Big Six" supermodels of the same period. Jennifer, choosing to show off her best assets—her legs—had chosen a silver slinky number that hid most of her goods at the top but barely covered her butt. She paired that with a bright red pump to accent her outfit. Robin opted for a slightly more classic get-up, wearing a royal blue pant jumpsuit that hung loose on her five-foot-nine body but dipped low in the front like the infamous JLo dress from the Grammys. With that, she wore silver strappy sandals that took her fifteen minutes to buckle. Rebecca, standing five foot six like Jennifer, wore a black-and-white strapless mini dress that pushed up her B-cup breasts and platform black Mary Janes, making her legs appear extra-long, especially next to me.

I'd decided to really test the waters and do something I hadn't in a while—rock a short pink spaghetti-strapped dress that showed off both my legs and my cleavage. It was a break against my cardinal rule of only showcasing one body asset at a time, but I'd lost a few pounds since going to spin class with Rebecca twice a week for the past couple months and was feeling myself. Plus, the dress wasn't *so* tight, so I figured that would take away some of the skank factor. In fact, it fit me like a corset at the top but flared out at the torso for a nice twirling effect at the hem, but the denouement was the way it complemented one of my favorite pairs of shoes: my nude platform sling-backs from Aldo. These shoes were perfect: sexy but simple, comfortable enough to wear for hours and they made me feel like a sassy diva ready to strut her stuff at the club.

Once in, I knew our first destination. The bar. But as we made our way through the crowd, I was quickly reminded of how packed clubs in DC could be on Friday nights and noticed the scores of people standing at the bar waiting for their drinks. There wouldn't be enough room for us all to head there together.

"Maybe I should go to the bar and get the drinks, and the rest of you find a spot for us somewhere?"

"That's not a bad idea," Robin replied, looking around to see how hard it might be to wrangle some space for us to gather. Everywhere she turned, in every corner of the club, people were standing tightly together. I could see her eyes get big as she scanned the area, but I also knew she had no desire to deal with the crowd at the bar and was all too happy to let me handle that part.

"You won't be able to carry four drinks on your own, though. I can come with," Rebecca offered.

"Okay, works for me," I said. "Tequila soda for you, Jenn, and rum and Coke for you, Rob?"

They both nodded their heads and walked away, determined to find us the perfect space—not too far from the rest of the clubgoers, but also not directly in the middle of the dance floor. It was certainly an art to doing so.

Rebecca and I were standing at the back of the crowd, waiting to get to the counter, when I faintly heard someone say something that sounded like it was directed to me. I thought I'd heard "What would you like to drink?" but that didn't seem quite right because we were nowhere near close enough for one of the bartenders to be asking us for our orders, and I hadn't perfected my "hey, come and flirt with me" face by that point of the night to illicit someone else offering to buy our drinks. Instead of responding, I turned back to Rebecca to confirm what she would want in case I got to the counter before she did. I also began slightly shifting my weight on my four-inch heels to see what pose felt the most comfortable; the shoes may have been made for dancing all night, but not standing still, lock-kneed for long periods of time.

"What would you like to drink?" came the question again, this time with a bit of a chuckle, and with a much clearer indication that it was, in fact, directed to me.

"I'm so sorry," I said, finally looking up and noticing the man who'd apparently noticed me a few moments earlier. "I didn't realize you were talking to me."

"It's cool." He smiled. "Hi."

Damn my addiction to men with straight white teeth. And great shoulders. And legs. *Oh, God, I'm staring*, I thought. But it was hard not to; this guy seemed like the kind of man who'd happily scoop you up as you melted in his arms.

"Hi," I said, trying to gain my composure. I was not going to let this man see me sweat, and I surely wouldn't let him know that in a matter of fifteen seconds I'd gone from distracted girl who didn't notice him to a girl who might ask him what *he* wanted to drink.

"Now that you know who I'm talking to, can I get you that drink?"

He spoke slowly and deliberately, not at all like what you would expect for someone to talk in a club. He didn't scream or try to outtalk the noise in the background. No, he spoke with the confidence and smoothness of a man who knew his whisper could be heard above anything, including the sounds of the beats stemming from the DJ's booth.

"Sure," I said, attempting to look the six-foot-plus chocolate drop of a man deep in his eyes. Even with my four-inch stilettos on, he beat me by a good four to five inches. "How about a whiskey ginger?"

He leaned closer to me, maybe to hear me better, maybe because the crowd was still building around us, or maybe just to torture me further. Either way, whatever his reason, I didn't want him to actually walk away to get the drink.

"Really? No Moscato? No champagne? A glass of Amaretto sour?" His smile grew bigger as he teased me, shining bright like he could have been a Colgate model at one point in his life.

"Nope, whiskey ginger is perfect."

"Wow, a beautiful woman who wants a whiskey ginger, huh? That's not a little girl's drink."

"I'm not a little girl," I said, trying to tease him back but swallowing the gulp in my throat.

"Hmm, well, then that means you might be able to hang with me. I like that."

"I guess that makes you a lucky guy," I said with a smile, trying my best not to jump him right then, but every time he grinned at me, it made it harder and harder. I stood on my tippy toes to try and get closer to his face. As the music grew around us, I peeked at my watch and noticed it was 11:00 p.m., just about the time DJs in DC thought the music should get louder and faster. It just so happened that this time around, the 808s were in lock step with my heartbeats.

"I guess it does," he said, inching in closer to me,

and bringing his voice to an even softer whisper. "A very, very lucky guy."

He stared at me. And smiled that big Colgate smile again. It was then that I knew I needed to pull myself together. I was all for the risk list and working to be vulnerable again, but that did not require me to be wide open with some stranger whose name I didn't even know yet.

But after only, maybe, five sentences, my legs were so weak, I couldn't stand on my toes any longer. Was it the heels or the man? Thinking it was the heels was easier to handle, so I slowly let my feet back down. This only caused him to lean in even closer to me.

"I'll be right back," he said. "Don't move."

He was just turning away from me when I suddenly remembered a very crucial detail: I wasn't meant to just be getting a drink for myself.

"Wait!" I called out and grabbed ahold of his nearest hand.

"Yes?"

"I just remembered I can't only get a drink for myself. I'm actually in line for my friends, too. So maybe you can just stand here with me while we wait?"

"Okay, I think I can do that." This time he was so close I could smell the hint of cologne on his neck. I didn't care that we'd just met; I wanted to know everything about this man, and possibly bury my head in his neck.

"Is that Pi cologne I smell?"

"Okay, you keep this up and I'm going to take you home and marry you tonight."

"What?" I asked jokingly. "I take it that means I'm right."

"Yes, you are indeed right." He watched me quizzically as if trying to study my face.

"How would you know that? You know what, never mind. Since you know something about me, how about you tell me something about you."

"Well, for starters, my name is Reagan," I said, placing my hand out to shake his. When we connected, I was pleasantly surprised by his firm grasp. Most guys tried to be too gentle with women, but he seemed to know just the right balance.

"I'm Luke."

"Nice to meet you, Luke."

"Same with you, Reagan," he said, finally dropping my hand. "So wait, as in Ronald Reagan?"

"Ugh, as in noble. Definitely not the former president."

"Don't pretend that's not a valid question."

"It's about as valid as me asking you if Luke is for Luke Perry."

"The 90210 guy?"

"Yeah."

"It's not, but now I wish it was. He was kind of a badass."

I blurted out laughing. "You're right, he was. But it's still not a valid question."

Inch by inch, we made our way closer to the counter to place our drink orders. I noticed that Rebecca was still off to the side of me a little, so I could potentially slide her the rest of the drinks if I wanted to spend a bit more time with Luke before meeting back up with the rest of the girls. Luke had obviously realized we were near as well, and that his time to close the deal was getting shorter and shorter. His charm offensive suddenly became much more apparent.

"So when we get these drinks, what do you say you give me just a little more time to get to know you before you meet back up with your friends?"

"I like the sound of that."

"Yeah?"

"Mmm-hmm." I bit my lower lip and looked him in his eyes. He seemed kind, even with his cockiness. Like he had a good story underneath the cool and confident demeanor he showed overtly.

We finally made it to the bar and placed our orders. As promised, I gave the other three drinks to Rebecca and told her I'd be over to her and the others in a little bit. She was all too happy to oblige, giving me the most obvious wink that I'd seen in ages.

"Now, this is a way to jump-start your risk list," she whispered in my ear before leaving me.

Oh, God, I hope Luke hadn't heard that.

I slowly turned back to him, and all I could see was his grin and his outstretched hand.

"Come with me."

I took a huge gulp of my drink and placed my

hand in his. We walked hand in hand until we reached a really crowded part of the club. At that point Luke positioned me in front of him so he could direct me from behind, his hand that once held mine slightly cupping my butt cheek and sending waves of pleasure down my spine.

Within minutes we'd found an empty place on a wall—just big enough for me to stand near it and for Luke to stand before me, enveloping me with his presence and height. I didn't know if it was the liquid courage, my desire to remove all thoughts of Jake from earlier, or just the way I was craving Luke all on his own, but I was suddenly pretty ramped up and feeling quite sexual.

"Reagan," he said, staring deep into my eyes. He leaned over me, put one hand on the wall behind me and used the other to cup his drink. Even with my heels, he still towered over me, which meant he had to lean closer in for us to talk, and it meant our lips were barely inches apart as he called my name.

"Yes," I answered breathlessly.

"A gender-neutral name for a pretty girl who likes manly drinks. There's so many things about you that make me want to know more."

I couldn't help the smile forming on my face. It had been quite some time since I'd felt this kind of chemistry with someone from the start. Probably since Jake. And back then I was way more willing to just throw myself out there, heart be damned. The guys since were all sexy and interesting enough to last a few months, but they never really wanted to know me. Maybe that was what instantly drew me to Luke. He had playboy charmer written all over him, but his words were different. *Maybe there was something to being open and the universe sending you what you wanted?*

"Tell me one thing you want to know besides why I like whiskey gingers and how I knew your cologne."

"I want to know what makes you happy."

He said the words so quickly, it caught me off guard. It was almost like he truly meant it, or really awful feeling alert: he was just *that* good. "I can't begin to tell you all of that in a club," I responded, trying to distract myself from the red flag rearing its ugly head inside.

"That's true, but you asked me what I wanted to know. Not what I wanted to know that you could tell me right now."

"Touché." I leaned my head down to mask my laughter. He was just as clever as he was attractive, obviously. "So what do you want to know that I can actually tell you here in the next five minutes?"

"Five minutes? That's all the time I get?"

"Afraid so. Anything more than that and you'll have to deal with the wrath of my friends. We came here to have a girls' night out tonight, and I've spent more time with you than them at this point."

"Fair. Okay, I want to know—" he stopped to let the suspense linger for a bit, knowing that made it sexier. Made him sexier "—how your lips taste. Can I know that?"

I nodded and closed my eyes as our lips connected and melted into each other. With his hands simultaneously roaming my body, Luke kissed me for what felt like hours of time floating in a cloud.

My gosh! My resolve was definitely wearing down. Thankfully, Luke took pity on me and stepped back to view his work on me, effectively ending the kiss and giving me just enough time to regain my composure.

"I think it's fair to say you know that now, yes?" I asked, clearing my throat.

"A little bit." He winked at me, and I could see he was truly enjoying himself and the effects he had on me. And that, something about him being able to have that much control over me, snapped me out of whatever desirable feelings I'd had previously and sent those red flags bouncing up again.

"You know, I think I know your type, Luke."

"And what type is that, Mr. President?"

"Playboy charmer, curious about the woman before him for a time, but that curiosity will eventually burn out. And you'll be gone as if you were never there."

"Wow, interesting theory of yours. What happens if you're wrong?"

"I haven't been yet," I replied, lightly biting my bottom lip and stretching my legs up so I could get myself in position to leave.

"You hadn't met me yet, either." There was a defiance in his voice but also compassion, like he knew why I was scared to let him in. But as much as I wanted to, I just couldn't do it. There was a reason all my senses were screaming loudly at me to run as fast and far away as I could. Sure, it could be fear. But it could just as easily be the result of learning my lessons, and I wasn't ready to risk which one it was that night.

"What do you say, pretty girl? Can I get your phone number? We can figure the rest of this out later."

"How about we make a deal," I countered, not wanting to say no to him, but not quite ready to say yes. "You find me again before you leave and it's all yours."

"Okay. Bet," he said, leaning into me once more. "I'm going to hold you to that, you know."

"We'll see." I scooched myself away from the wall, sliding past him, and began walking through the crowd to find my friends. But as he faded farther away from my sight, Rebecca's words rang loudly in my ear: I always run away when it gets scary, she'd said. Well, she was wrong. Apparently, I walked away, too.

It was 3:15 a.m. by the time I was back home and in the shower, attempting to wash the club off my body. Despite the hiccup with Luke, the rest of the night had actually been exactly what I needed: me and my girls dancing the night away, twerking and laughing for hours. The only thing left that I wanted was to get a great night's rest.

I stepped out of the shower and noticed I'd missed a text while I was in the bathroom. It was a message from Luke.

Hey Reagan, it's Luke. I ran into your homegirl who was with you at the bar, and she gave me your digits. I hope these are actually yours now that I think about it lol. HMB. I'd love to take you out for dinner. Give me a chance to prove you wrong.

I stared at my phone in shock. Of course, Rebecca would give him my number. I couldn't believe she wouldn't also give me a heads-up, but maybe that was the result of tequila brain. But now the question lingered about what I would do in response.

To give myself time to think, I finished drying off and getting ready for bed. Because I'd worn my natural curls tonight, I didn't bother wrapping my hair to make sure it would be straight in the morning. Instead, I pulled my hair into a ponytail and picked up my silk bonnet to put over my head for the night. With that in place, I put on a pair of gym shorts from college and a tank top, and then climbed into bed, staring at that message over and over, trying to assess the best way to control the situation.

Finally clear, I took a deep breath and responded:

Hi Luke, it's Reagan. Dinner sounds good.

I quickly pressed Send before I could chicken out, put my ringer on silent and placed my phone on the far end of my nightstand…as far away from my bed as I could get it. If I was ever going to get some rest, I needed to forget I sent that message and anything that might come from it.

Chapter Eight

When I woke up the next morning, I rolled over and reached for my phone, immediately freaking out about whether I should have replied to Luke last night. Maybe I should have waited until today when it was a more appropriate time to text? What if he took that to mean I wanted to see him last night on some booty call stuff? Or worse, what if I looked at my phone and there was nothing from him yet?

I turned the phone over and saw one missed text. From Luke. One minute after my reply last night. And all it read was: Yes!

It was a simple word, but that level of excitement from a guy this early on was refreshing. He used an exclamation point in a text, for goodness' sake. Most of the men I'd met were still trying to play it very cool to the chest in our first conversations, and there was Luke, unabashedly showing his excitement. It was admirable and really sexy. And it most certainly deserved a reply back.

I sat up in my bed and texted him back:

lol good morning. Sorry I missed your text last night; I crashed after my shower.

I leaned back onto my headrest and waited to see if he would respond back immediately. I was fully prepared to have to crawl back under my covers if minutes passed by while I waited, but thankfully, I didn't have to. It took less than a minute before I saw his number appear on my phone again.

All good.

I kind of figured.

What are you doing tonight?

In three separate texts, in less than fifteen words, Luke managed to not only calm down my nerves, but also ask me out again. The man *was* good.

Nothing in stone yet. Are you trying to get dinner already? I replied.

Not dinner, yet. But I was thinking you, me, a bunch of lights and some animals lol.

I sat up again in my bed, excited at the possibility he was referring to one of my favorite Christmas things to do in DC.

As in Zoo Lights? I asked.

Ha ha, yeah. You probably think that's corny, right?

No. I love it actually!

Now I'm the one responding with exclamation points, I thought. Was this contagious?

See? I knew there were things I liked about you, Reagan. Text me your address, and I'll pick you up at 6.

I dutifully did as I was told and slid back down into my bed. Something felt different about this guy, like maybe he wouldn't just be another notch in five-month-Betty's belt. Or maybe it was me who was different? I didn't know for sure; I just knew I was going on a date with him less than twenty-four hours after I'd made up my mind to never see him again. That was impressive. I pulled my comforter over my head to block out the sun that was beginning to invade my bedroom and screamed into my pillow. I was going on a date and could hardly contain my enthusiasm.

The neon, multicolored lights flanking the trees at the entrance to the Smithsonian's National Zoo were perfect in the evening, lighting up the sky and inciting joy for all the children and adults walking up to them. And Luke and I were no different. In fact, we might have been as excited as the kids who ran past us while we marveled at the glittery passageway lighting our way into the park with red, green, blue, yellow and orange lights above and around us. It was one of those sights where, if you stood there for a moment, you could get lost in the wonderment of it all…watching the lights twinkle under the moonlight and then catching them as they bounced off the skin of the man next to you.

I peeked over at Luke with a smile plastered on my face and saw that he was staring in awe just as much as I was. "When's the last time you came here?" I asked, tapping his hand to get his attention.

"Man, it's been a while. Maybe three, four years. I don't remember it being like this."

"You've been in DC that long?"

"Yeah. I came here fresh out of college five years ago, wanting to make a difference in the nation's capital."

"Ahhh, so that's why you became a teacher. Altruistic goals."

"What can I say? I've got a heart of gold." He grinned at me to show he was joking, at least a little bit. "What about you? What drew you to writing about politics?"

"DC did, actually," I replied as we began walking through the rest of the zoo. "I always knew I wanted to be a writer. It was the thing that remained a constant for me as a little girl, even as my parents divorced and everything changed about our family dynamic. All of a sudden, I had three little siblings looking to me to be an example for them on what to do at all times. And I never knew anything, except that I could write. It took living here to help me figure out what I wanted to say, though."

"Wow. That was probably a lot to handle. I'm sorry you felt so much pressure as a young girl."

"It doesn't go away, honestly. I still feel it all the time, even now with my brother at twenty-six and my sisters at twenty-two and seventeen. I feel like I have to constantly be perfect for them. It's part of why I like living so far away. I get to make mistakes without them knowing about it."

"Well, I'm glad you're here, too. And you can make all the mistakes you want with me," he said with a wink. "Plus, this place just has an effect on people, you know? Once you're here, like you said, you realize how much politics is in every single fiber of our lives, whether we realize it or not."

"Exactly. I usually have to try to explain that to people. It's nice to hear someone say it to me, instead."

"Told you, girl. I'm going to prove you wrong if it's the last thing I do."

"I see."

Luke grabbed my hand, and we continued strolling until we came upon one of the new glowing animal lanterns: a lion family perched regally next to an LED-powered tree. The power that exuded from these lanterns was astounding. It was almost as if we were watching the real thing, with the way they stood and the attention to detail that was given to everything from the dad lion's hair to the expressions on their faces.

"So beautiful, right?" I turned back to Luke to see if I would catch him in awe again. I'd loved seeing the look on his face when we first walked in; it was like a kid who first tastes chocolate cake. They are all at once in awe, but also trying to figure out where this amazingness has been all their lives. But this time he wasn't watching the attractions in the zoo. His eyes were squarely on me.

"Yes, you are," he said.

"Luuuuke!" I playfully slapped him on his shoulder. "Turn down the cool factor for me. We're still getting to know each other." I immediately regretted my last statement when I saw his shoulders slump down a little before he could catch himself and hide his expression of disappointment. It didn't last long, however; within seconds he'd recovered and was back to charmer Luke. But I'd seen a glimpse of what a dent in his armor looked like, and felt horrible to have caused it, even if just for a moment.

"Never mind," he said. "You know what? Let's play a game of Truth or Dare."

"Okay," I said hesitantly, but after my last hiccup I didn't want to seem like I was scolding him again.

"All right, you go first. Truth or dare?"

"Definitely truth."

"Do you like me, Reagan?"

"Wow, no start-up questions, huh?"

"Nah," he chuckled. "I think you know by now I don't do things at Level One."

"That I do. From you kissing me in the club to texting me out of the blue to our first date in less than twenty-four hours. I'd say that's definitely not Level One."

"Exactly. So stop stalling and answer the question."

"Yeah, I… I think so. As much as I can like someone in such a short period of time."

"Mmm-hmm," he said, scrunching his face at me.

"I wouldn't be here if I didn't like something about you, Luke. You are intriguing, for sure. And very sexy, but you already know that."

He bent down so his face could be next to mine, and I could see the smirk on his face from my periphery as I tried to avoid his eyes. "That's a really long answer to avoid saying yes, Mr. President."

"I said yes at the beginning. I just explained it a little, that's all."

"Whatever you say."

"What about you? Do you like me, Luke Perry?" Since he'd apparently deemed *Mr. President* his nickname for me, I figured it was only right I also sometimes called him by his not-namesake as well. Plus, I needed something to get some leverage back into this conversation that was equally jokey but also kind of intense.

"Nope. You have to ask truth or dare first."

"Ugh, fine. Truth or dare?"

"Dare," he answered with a smirk, purposely choosing the opposite of what he knew I wanted from him.

"I dare you to do the Zootube slide," I said, pointing to the slides that spanned the length of the lion exhibit, mimicking snow tube slides found in ski resorts across the country.

"On one condition."

"You can't have conditions on Truth or Dare!"

"Sure, you can. My condition is that you slide on the one next to me."

I glanced at him for a beat and contemplated how hard I wanted to press that you could not, in fact, create conditions around Truth or Dare. Problem was I did want to get on the slide, too, so he'd put me in a position where I both wanted to disagree with him and wanted to say yes. Placing my hand on his shoulder, I looked him dead in his eyes and said the only thing I could say: "Deal."

He grinned with satisfaction.

"But if I beat you, I get to skip my next turn and you have to answer truth next time around."

"I'm not afraid of you, Reagan. Let's do it." He removed my hand from his shoulder and shook it with that same firm grip from the night before. And then the race was on. We both took off running to the slides. I was thankful I'd chosen to wear my midnight black, flat, thigh-high boots instead of heels.

Not only were they the perfect touch for turning jeans and a blouse into a sexy outfit, there was also no way I could have run anywhere with any of the three-inch-plus stilettos in my closet.

"On your mark," I said as we both climbed into our tubes and prepared to be pushed by the zoo employees.

"Get set," he screamed back at me.

"Go!"

Off we both went down the slide, screaming like we were on the world's largest roller coaster and not the little kid slides that had been erected to introduce some interactive fun at the zoo. I hopped out of my tube as fast as I could and ran to him.

"I won! I won!"

"That you did," he said, laughing and trying to climb out of his own tube. With his long legs, he was having a hard time getting out on his own, so I reached out my hand to help him up. As soon as he grabbed me, we both went soaring feet away from the slides. I was amazed neither of us fell onto the ground, but I think just when we were about to, he caught me midair and steadied us both.

"Okay, so a deal is a deal. Truth. Do you like me?"

"I can't believe you wasted your truth on something you already know."

"Maybe a girl needs to hear it sometimes."

"Reagan Doucet, I will tell you all day long how much I like you," he said, bending down again so he could stare directly into my eyes. "But you have to believe me when I do. No more of that 'c'mon, Luke' stuff. You either believe me or you don't."

"Deal," I said, grabbing ahold of the loops on the waist of his pants to bring him even closer to me. "You got it."

"Mmm, no. I've got you," he whispered, bringing his lips centimeters away from mine but refusing to kiss me. Instead, he stood there, making me wait, and then flicked out his tongue with a grin, barely scraping the skin on my lips. It was clear Luke wanted me to want him. Better yet, crave him. And while I could also tell this was him putting on his charm armor again, I didn't care. I was in shoe, Christmas lights and sexy guy heaven, and for once I was determined to enjoy it. Not much could top that.

"Now, let's go find these pandas."

I reached out my hand, and he took it as we went skipping to the next exhibit.

Chapter Nine

"You should try some of this salad."

"The salad made of seaweed?" I asked, scrunching my face.

"Yes, that one," Luke laughed. "C'mon, it'll be great. I promise."

"Okay, sure. Why not," I said, first hesitating and then relenting to his persistence. In a weird way, that was sort of indicative of me and Luke anyway. His persistence in getting my number from Rebecca after I snubbed him caused me to give him another look and rethink my position on his charmer, playboy ways. And in just six weeks, even with the Christmas holiday interrupting us, he was already doing a pretty good job of convincing me that my first impression may have been off. Maybe that would be the case with this seaweed salad, too.

He dipped his fork into his bowl and twirled around a tiny portion of the seaweed before lifting his eyes back up and bringing the fork to my mouth. "What do you think?" he asked as I chewed on the dish.

I think it's hilarious you just fed me, I thought to myself, *especially considering how intimate that is*. But since I'd learned that Luke was the kind of guy who enjoyed being open and vulnerable, including wanting to do intimate, if slightly uncomfortable things, like feeding me in the middle of a crowded Thai restaurant, I did not say what I was really thinking.

"It's actually not bad," I replied.

"Not bad?"

"Yes, not bad." I burst out laughing at how upset he was that I didn't fall out for his seaweed. If only he knew what my original reply was going to be.

"And by *not bad*, you obviously mean best salad you've ever had, right?"

"Not quite, Luke Perry," I said, laughing. "But if it makes you feel better, it's a lot tastier than some of the food you've cooked for me so far."

"Wow, that stings, Mr. President. For real?" Like a little kid, he held another piece of seaweed salad on his fork, and I could almost see his desire to flick it at me oozing off him. If we were at either of our homes, I'd be toast by now, seaweed flying through the air in my direction. "You know you like my cooking. C'mon, you can admit it," he added, taunting me with that fork across the table.

"Me? Like your cooking?"

"Yes," he laughed. "You."

"I think... I liked maybe *one* of the meals you made, but I'm not sure I can speak to your cooking as a whole just yet." I looked back at him with a smug smile. *Two could play his taunting game.*

"It didn't seem like that when you were in the clean-plate club for the last three."

"Oh, right," I replied, pausing to pretend as if I was considering his counterargument. "You do make a good point. So maybe I enjoy your cooking just a little bit. Like this much." I used my right hand to show a tiny space between my pointer finger and thumb.

"Oh, just that much, huh?"

"Wellll, okay. Maybe this much." I opened the space between my fingers to about the size of a ballpoint pen.

"I don't know if you know this, but—" he sucked his teeth before continuing "—that's still not all that great, babe."

"Oh? It's not? Hmm, maybe I meant this much?" This time I used both hands to show the space between them, giving about a ruler's length in between as my description.

Luke leaned across the table, drawing himself

closer to me so that his hand could almost touch me if he wanted to.

"I'm still not completely sold on this appreciation yet."

"No? Darn. Well, what do you say about this much?" I winked and spread my arms, open wide, just in time for him to sneak over and begin tickling me, causing me to have a laughing fit in the middle of the restaurant.

"Wait, wait, wait," I said in between uncontrollable giggles.

He paused briefly, allowing me to pant out a paltry "No fair!" right before tickling me some more.

"Sorry, sweetheart. All's fair in love and war," he said, winking at me like a man who'd just won the night.

"This isn't over."

"Yeah, yeah, we'll see. Maybe you'll have a better chance when you come visit me in New Orleans."

"Ugh, don't remind me." I sat back into my chair, my mood completely changing from the jovial joking one to one of sadness. It took three dates and a Christmas break for Luke to tell me that, of all the times for us to meet, we met just as he was getting ready to move away from DC. At the time he told me, I was ready to call it quits, but then he said the one thing I'd wanted Jake to say all those years before: "Reagan, the moment I saw you standing at that bar, I knew I had to meet you, potential long distance be damned."

How could I resist him when he was willing to fight for me after only a few weeks? That was not to say the revelation had been easy, but we both hoped that his moving to my hometown would make things slightly better to manage.

"Don't pout, pretty girl. This is our last dinner together before I move. I don't want it to be sad."

"I don't, either. And I'm trying not to make it that way, I promise. I just…can't stop thinking about how hard it's going to be."

"You don't think it's damn near fate-like that I'm moving to where you're from, of all places?" He reached over the table again to hold my hand as he spoke.

"That is pretty freaky," I replied with a grin starting to grow back on my face.

"Exactly."

"But," I reminded him, "that doesn't change the fact that I live in DC now, and New Orleans is thousands of miles away from here. I may be from there, but I get to go home maybe three or four times a year, max. That doesn't sound like the makings of a great relationship."

"It can be. I can come up here three or four times a year, too. And then before you know it, it's only a little over a month in between the times we get to see each other in person."

"And that sounds ideal to you?"

"No, of course not. But you're worth it."

There he went again, saying words I wasn't quite sure I believed, even though I desperately wanted to.

"And you're already coming home for Mardi Gras in a couple weeks."

"Yes, I am," I said with a sigh, already sensing that once again his persistence was wearing me down. "And you're going to meet my family. Are you ready for that?"

"Nothing can be more intense than meeting Robin and Jennifer, so I think I'm good."

"That's true. They did put you through the wringer."

"Yeah, but they also said something to me about a list you're working on?"

I almost spit my food out of my mouth. Had they told him that he was potentially a check on it when I hadn't said anything to him yet?

"List? What list did they tell you about?" I asked.

"I don't know. Just something about how they thought you might be buying a new pair of shoes soon to check off a thing on it."

"Ahhhh, well. It's not, like, literal. Just something where I'm keeping track of stuff that I want to do more," I said, trying to find the best words so I didn't offend him and have him thinking he was just part of some game.

"And I'm one of those things you want to do more?" He licked his lips and raised his eyebrow toward me. "Maybe more of what we did the other night?"

"Not like that, silly. Just in terms of me being more open with someone like you."

"Okay. I like the sound of that. And the shoes? Why are you buying a new pair of shoes?"

"The shoes are just for the ball, babe," I said, lying. I wasn't ready to get into the intricacies of how the shoes were my reward for the list I'd just told him wasn't real.

"Now, that makes sense and sounds like the Reagan I know." He moved his hand closer to me and began lightly tickling me again.

"Whatever," I said, playfully slapping his hand away.

"But for real, we're going to make it, okay?"

"Okay. I trust you." And maybe in some small way, I actually was beginning to.

My visit home for the last week of Mardi Gras started off no differently than it did whenever I went down there with the addition of a few parades. I'd been home for a few days, spending most of my time either with Luke or my family, when before I knew it, my last night was upon us. And while I didn't want to leave, I woke up that morning with an air of expectancy all around me. It had been years since I'd made it home during Mardi Gras, and that night I would be attending one of the famed carnival balls along with my mom and some of my other family members.

I rose out of bed with an extra pep in my step,

made sure to lay out the dress I was wearing that night—a floor-length royal purple gown that cinched at my midsection and flowed downward with ease— and pulled out the heels that would accent my outfit. Sure, I had my mask and jewelry as well, but c'mon, this was always going to be all about the shoes. The girls had almost let the cat slip out of the bag, but the truth was I had been thinking about buying a new pair of shoes, not for the ball, but to symbolize me finally being open to love again. Luke had gone from a cute and sexy guy in the club one night to meeting my friends and making me reconsider all the notions I'd had previously about men, trusting them and putting my heart on the line. We'd even talked about him meeting my family when he picked me up from the ball. This was insanely fast for my normal timeline, but if I was going to take the plunge into trusting love again, letting him meet them as we left seemed like the perfect compromise. We could spend about ten minutes laughing with everyone and then have the rest of the night to ourselves.

When it came time to get ready, I carefully put my dress on, took my pin curls down to let my hair fall past my shoulders, meticulously applied my makeup and then stepped into quite possibly my new favorite shoes—a pair of gold lamé heels that made just the right statement. You could see the sparkle of the lamé from the front and the shine of the gold-plated heel from the back. They were, to put it in one word, heavenly.

Unfortunately, they were not the best-feeling shoes with their five-inch stiletto heel and barely a platform style, but at that moment it didn't matter. I hadn't been to a Mardi Gras ball since I was seventeen, and on this night I wanted to be sure that I would sparkle and shine. Plus, I also knew that at midnight, Luke would be coming to pick me up from the ball so that we could spend the rest of my last night together.

This night was like my own little version of Cinderella coming true! The biggest difference? I didn't have the ugly stepsisters and stepmother trying to make my ball experience a downer, and midnight would be when I got to spend time with my prince, instead of the other way around. So I guess it was like the opposite of Cinderella, but with those shoes I felt like the belle of the ball.

Before we left the house, I looked around to check out how good my family looked in their outfits. My mom stood five foot nine, with her black-and-gold gown flowing to the floor, slightly tickling the kitten heels she had on underneath. Her olive skin tone perfectly matched the gold accents and accessories she wore that night, giving her a flawless glow. But she wasn't the only one who would be stopping cars in the street; the rest of my family looked just as good and debonair with their suits and gowns, too. My youngest sister, Charlie, wowed in my old red mermaid gown from college, and her best friend sparkled in a yellow dress that had hints of gold in it, too. I even caught some of the guys straightening their bow ties on their immaculately tailored tuxedos and making sure their shoes were buffed to perfection. We looked good! Right before we walked out the door, I slid on my grandmother's faux mink coat that had been passed down through the Chevaliers to my mom and then to me, picked up my mask, and we made our way to the New Orleans Convention Center.

At the ball, the place was filled with beads and masks, confetti and doubloons, massive spreads of food and liquor overflowing. I saw plenty of happy faces talking as they waited for the parade to enter in. Everyone seemed to be enjoying the debauchery of just being alive. We were in New Orleans during Carnival after all, so there was nothing to do but to live it up. There was dancing and drunk singing, loud laughter and complete disregard for everything outside those four walls. And once the parade floats poured in with beads flying everywhere, you could see gala patrons drunkenly swinging the beads around after they caught them. Music from the brass band blared through the ballroom, enticing everyone to keep the party going and let the music take control of their limbs. It was a sight to see. At least for everyone but me.

Sure, I was having a great time—more than a blast, really—but I'd also silently begun my countdown to midnight. While for most people, the ball wouldn't be over until about 4:00 a.m., I was looking forward to my shortened experience, because that meant more time with my man. I kept thinking of the moment he would see me when he walked through those doors, and his breath would be caught somewhere deep in his throat. Truthfully, I also couldn't wait to be in his arms again and feel his hands all over me, especially when it would be another month or two before we'd see each other.

My mom could sense my excitement as well. "He's going to be blown away when he sees you tonight," she said. "You are absolutely stunning." *Nothing like a confidence boost from your mom, right?*

"But you know, that's not for another few hours." Maria ended her statement by slightly raising her eyebrows and giving me a very knowing look.

Leave it to my mom to make her point without saying too much. Her words helped snap me out of my Luke trance, though, and I realized that I still had another two hours before I would see him. I finally lost myself in the fun that was surrounding me, drinking champagne and becoming one of the people making loud sounds of laughter. No longer an onlooker, I danced and tipsily sang songs like "Another One Bites the Dust" and "Low Places," while simultaneously calling out to the float riders to "Throw me something, mister!"

"I'm so glad you're here tonight, Rae," my mom said as she handed an enormous set of beads to me. "I only wish I could see my babies more often. Charlie and I miss you, your brother and sister…just leaving us and spreading out to cities all over the country."

"I am, too, Mommy," I said, ignoring her patented passive-aggression again. "And I'm glad you reminded me that I should be enjoying myself while I'm here."

"Did I do that?" she asked, knowing full well she did.

"Uhhhh, yeah," I laughed.

"If I said anything at all, it was only out of love, *cher*." She winked at me in the way she always did when she knew her ways had worked.

We continued on, reveling in the joyous occasion, jumping around and dancing and maybe even spilling the champagne we were drinking, but definitely laughing with our whole bodies for the next two hours. At 11:50 p.m., everything stopped for me, and I began to prepare myself for midnight. Luke and I had already talked about how he would meet me in front at that time, so there was no need to check in. Still, I took my phone out of my purse anyway—you know, just in case. I kissed my family goodbye, slid my coat back on and made my way to the front door.

I walked out to the lobby of the convention center and impatiently waited, tapping my shoes on the floor and looking around for my beau. I also practiced my poses and daydreamed about what he would say when he saw me. I thought about how he would react. Would he scoop me up in his arms and twirl me around or just stand there in awe? Would he kiss me as soon as he saw me or wait until we walked back to his car? We'd been dating for a couple months at this point, but he'd never seen me dressed up like this, and I just knew he was going to be in for a good surprise.

After twenty minutes of still no prince, I began to worry. He hadn't called or picked up the phone when I called. He hadn't shown up when he said he would. He hadn't even texted to let me know if something had changed. But I knew how much Luke liked me, so I tried not to panic that something had happened to him on his way to come get me.

It wasn't easy, however. And my brain kept coming up with the worst possible scenarios. What if he'd gotten into a car accident on his way to get me, and he was somewhere lying in a ditch, calling out for help but no one could hear him? What if he'd been kidnapped and thrown into the river because someone mistook him for some other smooth, dark-skinned guy who just so happened to be in the mob? What if a friend of his had gotten really sick and he'd had to rush him to the hospital and there was no time to call me to let me know he'd have to cancel?

All kinds of scenarios ran through my head. And as each minute passed, they progressively got worse. I mean, what could be so wrong that he couldn't pick up the phone?

I looked at my phone again and saw it read 12:30 a.m. Thirty minutes and no call. I dialed his number again. *Ring. Ring. Ring.* A gazillion rings and still no answer.

I dialed again.

And again.

And again.

And again.

There was no denying I was in full panic mode at this point. Sweat was beginning to drip down the sides of my head. My heart was racing. My palms were so sweaty, my fingers could barely make the contact to press his name on my phone.

And then a sudden, heartbreaking feeling hit me deep in the pit of my stomach. What if he'd just decided not to come?

With that last question, I stopped calling and slid my phone back into my purse. I didn't have the energy to walk back into the ballroom, however; instead, I decided to just stand on the wall for a little longer.

Finally, at 12:45 a.m., I felt my phone vibrating through my purse. I caught my breath, reached inside and answered before even looking at the screen. Something inside me already knew it was him. And it was. He was calling to tell me that he wasn't coming. That he'd gone by a friend's house to hang out instead. That he'd been thinking about it, and maybe it was best that we just ended it that night instead of dragging out the long distance further. That maybe we'd moved too fast too soon, and he wasn't ready to come to an event with my family attending. That

he was sorry he didn't say something earlier. That...
Honestly, the rest of what he said really didn't matter anymore. I hung up the phone, shell-shocked, not quite sure what had just happened and dejected that I would have to walk back into the ball and admit to everyone that I'd never left. Disappointed in the knowledge that this was surely the end for us. That my last thought had come true; he'd really just simply chosen not to come. I couldn't believe he'd chosen this moment to make a fool of me.

I walked back into the hall to everyone's surprise, making the statement entrance I'd intended for earlier in the evening, my shoes sparkling even while the light in my eyes dimmed. There I was. Cinderella. Stood up at midnight. It was surely a sight to see.

"*Cher*, is everything okay?" my mom asked as she came running up to me, her hair flying behind her like a superwoman cape.

"Yeah, I don't really want to talk about it."

"Are you sure?"

"Yep, I'm sure." I walked past her, my head down, attempting desperately to hold my tears in. *This isn't anything new*, I reminded myself. One thing I could always count on was the other shoe dropping as soon as things seemed to be going too well, especially with the men in my life. Time and time again it happened, and Luke had been no different.

When I arrived back at our table, I quietly slid off the heels that had now become constricting to my feet and exchanged them for my comfy ballet slippers. There was no need to keep playing the part. The ball was over. I'd been stood up by the man who was supposed to be my Prince Charming. Those damned shoes seemed more cursed than favorites.

Chapter Ten

"Alexa, play Ariana Grande's *Thank U, Next* album on shuffle."

I took one huge gulp from my wineglass and breathed in deeply, preparing myself as I waited for the music to begin. To say it had been an excruciating past eighteen hours would be putting it lightly. After being embarrassed in front of my family, I then had to endure the next several hours of questions and attempts of people being comforting that just fell flat every time. There was nothing they could say to me that would make me feel better, because it was my fault for thinking that things would be different with Luke than with any other man in my life. Jake left me. Matthew cheated on me. Countless other guys either ghosted, bread crumbed, or laughed at me falling off a damn bed.

All I really wanted was to get back here, back to my apartment, so I could kick off the combat boots I wore on the plane, blast my music, sing and dance and scream around my place until I was worn out and then go to sleep.

As the intro to "In My Head" began playing, I took another swig of wine before helping Ariana belt out the tragic tale of a woman who fell in love with someone who was only amazing in her dreams. Instinctively, my arms began to sway and feet started to move on beat. It wasn't long before I'd danced my way into my closet, my safe haven when things got really hard to handle. Everyone always teased me about how much I loved my shoe closet, but nothing in there had ever disappointed me. I could put on a pair of any of the shoes surrounding me, and they would instantly make me feel better, help me stand taller, remind me who I was and to never let the pain sit too long before I sucked it up and moved on.

The only problem was in my closet was also my shoe diary, and inside my diary was that damn risk list. The song changed, and I twirled around in my closet for the first verse, letting the music speak to my soul, closing my eyes and taking it all in. I was done, I thought to myself. Done with the risks, done with the men, done with it all, because each time it didn't work out, it was too painful, too heartbreaking and too devastating. And I was tired of encouraging myself to get back up just to get hurt again.

I picked up my diary and stared at the list I'd written four months before in my blue pen because I'd had some sense of hope that day, even despite the doubts I had. There was no hope anymore. Just frustration and finally, resolve. I tore the page out of the diary, crumpled it up and leaned out of my closet so I could throw it into the trash can in my room. If I'd learned anything from the past couple days, it was a reminder that safe might be boring, and it might not get the kudos from your friends, but it felt a whole lot better than this.

Turning back around to my shoes, I breathed in deeply again and began looking for what shoes I'd wear to work tomorrow. I'd need something to give me an extra pep in my step when I told Peter I was finally accepting his promotion offer.

At work the next day I sat at my desk and furiously typed on my laptop, earphones in to try to avoid any questions from Rebecca about how things had gone on my trip home. In my peripheral I saw her repeatedly turn to me and think about interrupting me, slightly leaning in but each time, ultimately changing her mind. I knew she was curious, but we also had a long-standing pact that when either of us had earphones in, it meant we were head down in a project and should be disturbed for emergency purposes only. We'd always respected that pact, but I could tell she must have been torn on whether my trip constituted an emergency or not. After all, I'd walked in and barely said a word to her before sitting down and immediately burying my nose into my computer.

She finally decided to message me on our company instant messenger.

I know what earphones mean, but just making sure you're all right.

Yeah, I'm good. Just busy, I replied. The truth was I didn't want to answer questions or have to tell her I was waiting on Peter to come in so that I could accept the promotion offer. I knew she'd try to talk me out of it if I did, and I'd already made up my mind. But I was far too chicken to handle any probing from her in the meantime. Can you let me know if you see Peter come in, though? Need to talk to him.

Sure.

Thanks.

I went back to pretending like I had the biggest breaking story on the way when really I was just going over in my mind some of the topics that I thought might be good for my vertical and what stories and content I would want to roll it out with. *I'd love to get some really great quotes from various women in politics, media and pop culture and have them to pepper throughout the week as new content*, I thought. One thing I knew from working to raise my profile on Instagram around my shoes was that the more content you released, if it was compelling and people could count on it consistently, the more viewers and followers you got. And it didn't need to always be long, drawn-out content. A quote here, an image there, even the right video could keep my readers coming back while I worked on features to deliver to them every week.

He's here.

A little after 10:00 a.m. I saw Rebecca's message come across my screen. *Peter is nothing, if not consistent*, I said to myself.

Thanks, Becs! Really appreciate it.

No problem.

I saved my work, took my earphones out and stood up from my seat, sliding my silver-studded, black "smoking loafers" back on. At some point they'd slipped off the heels of my feet while I was typing, and I hadn't stopped to fix them at the time. Out of the corner of my eye, I saw Rebecca studying me to figure out what was going on, an act she continued even as I walked past her. She seemed even more confused when I winked at her as I awkwardly tried to comfort her clear concerns without actually using my voice.

"Hey, Peter, you have a second?" I was maybe a minute behind him when he'd walked into his office, so I initially peeked in to at least give the impression like I wasn't stalking him.

"I already know Rebecca alerts you when I come in," he said as he placed his briefcase down on the floor and sat down in his seat.

"What? I don't know what you're talking about."

"Sure, sure, Reagan. What's up? How can I help you?"

"Well," I said, stepping fully into his office and cracking the door behind me. "I wanted to officially see if your offer was still on the table for my own vertical."

"Yes, absolutely," he said, sitting up in his seat. "I've been waiting for you to get back to me on this, rather patiently might I add, but I'm glad you finally decided to say yes."

"I'm sorry about the delay. It's just between Christine and then the break for the holidays and…" I stopped myself before I added any more details like being stood up in front of my entire family.

"I understand completely. That's why I hadn't pushed you. Plus, you've still been delivering on your normal content. Your opinion piece on the ways Senators Warren and Klobuchar were pitted against each other in the Democratic primary was gold the other day. This promotion really is because I believe you've earned the opportunity to be our leading voice on women and politics."

"Thank you, Peter. Truly."

"Don't mention it." He leaned back in his chair and reached into his desk to pull out a stack of papers before handing them to me. "Now's the fun part. You have to fill out all this paperwork for HR for it to go into effect. You do that today, and I'll make sure it all goes through pretty quickly. You could be up and running beginning of April if we're lucky."

"That would be amazing," I said, that much happier I'd taken the time this morning to work on the beginnings of an internal production schedule. "I'll be sure to fill these out today and let you know when I'm done."

I stepped farther into Peter's office and took the stack of papers from him, then turned on my feet and began walking back out to get to my desk. *See?* I thought. *The risk list might not have gotten me this at another job.* Sometimes it took staying where you were to get where you wanted to be.

Halfway down the hallway, I turned around again when I heard Peter calling my name.

"Yes?" I asked, looking at him quizzically.

"Sorry," he said, attempting to catch his breath. I imagined he'd run out of his office to try to catch me, thinking I was farther away than I actually was. "In all the excitement, I forgot to mention a couple parameters around the vertical, since you know, this is your first one and all."

"Sure, that's understandable." I stood facing him, my hands clutching the papers he'd just given me and wishing he'd either remembered these parameters in his office or waited to talk to me at my desk. In the middle of the hallway was kind of weird, but I'd go along with it. As if he could sense my apprehension to the location, he started walking with me to my desk, his breath now back to normal.

"The first thing is I'll need to see an initial list of the topics you're thinking of covering so I can be sure we're on the same page about what the vertical is intended to do."

"Of course. I was actually working on that this morning. I think I have some ideas that will really help increase our audience, especially among young women who aren't largely targeted by political on-line magazines."

"Great, that sounds great. I'm also going to want you to finally add our email app to your phone and also to send me a list of the potential people you're thinking of interviewing or including in your first posts."

With each step we took closer to my desk, the *parameters* as he'd called them grew more and more restricting. I'd assumed the first two were probably part of the deal. But the last one felt like it meant more was coming with it. I turned to Peter to stop our progress and look at him face-to-face, no longer caring where we were in the building. "Is there something you're not telling me, Peter? Just a minute ago you were telling me that I earned this opportunity, so I thought that meant you trusted my judgment as a valuable staff writer over the past four years. Why does it seem like you're hesitant now?"

"I wouldn't say hesitant, Reagan. I just know that you are really excited, and I applaud that, but I also want to make sure that even as we're thinking of expanding our audience, we're true to this site's current audience," he said. "It doesn't help us to get younger, more diverse readers if we lose the people who built our readership in the first place."

"Honestly, Peter. I think that's a misunderstanding of who reads my articles on our site," I countered. "But I get it. Don't go too radical too fast is what you're saying."

"Your words, not mine, Reagan," he said. "But yes."

I watched him as he walked back to his office, steadying my breathing once again, but this time to calm my frustration. *So much for the ideas I was working on earlier*, I thought. When I opened my eyes and turned back around, I suddenly realized just how close we'd gotten to my desk before I'd stopped him. And there was Rebecca, sitting in her chair, staring at me with disgust. It was clear she'd not only overheard the conversation, but she also thought it was a load of crap.

She was not wrong.

I spent the next few hours continuing to avoid Rebecca, filling out my paperwork and desperately trying to tweak my earlier ideas into what I thought might be more palatable for Peter. Gone were the plans for developing hashtags, posting memes and using things like music lyrics over the decades to show the progression, and sometimes regression, of women in American society. Instead, I replaced those ideas with more prototypical ones, such as exploring maternal mortality rates in light of health care discussions being such a point of contention in the Democratic primary. I kept in my desire for interviewing influential women and using pop quotes as intermediate content, but I replaced potential interviewees like Austin Channing Brown, the amazing author of *I'm Still Here*, with women more conventionally viewed as being in politics.

By the time I was done, Rebecca had gone home, as had many of the other employees at our job. She'd messaged me after observing the fiasco with Peter and simply said we could talk later, because she knew I probably didn't want to at that moment. I appreciated her grace, because I wasn't sure I would have been able to keep my composure if I'd actually started expressing myself out loud. I felt the anger tears trying to surface when I'd sat back down, and the one good thing about having to rework all of my ideas was that it gave me enough incentive and distraction to stuff all those feelings and do what I needed to do. After all, I'd chosen this promotion, and I was going to do my damnedest to try to make the best of it.

I reread my plans once more to check for spelling errors or any potential hiccups that might give Peter heartburn and then sent him my email. After closing my laptop, I took a brief moment for myself and enjoyed the quiet in the office. No *click-clacks* of heels or friends to avoid, just peace and silence. I could have probably stayed there for longer if not for the vibration I heard stemming from my phone.

Oh, goodie, I thought, picking it up and noticing it was my first official email alert on my phone from work. From Peter.

Reagan, great ideas so far. I like the direction you're heading in. Let's talk some more tomorrow.

"Of course you do, Peter," I said underneath my breath. I'd built it to be the perfect amount of me, but with slightly less soul. That could work for now, but I was going to have to figure out how to slyly bring back in some of my *radical* ideas or I'd drive myself crazy.

Chapter Eleven

The next morning I awoke reinspired. I'd spent most of the evening pouting, and then needing a respite, so I went scrolling through my Instagram and Twitter feeds. That was when it hit me. Peter and I didn't have to be on opposing sides. The reality was that I wanted to write the stories that were more conventionally around women and politics. There wasn't anything on the ideas list I shared with him that made me cringe or feel like I was being asked to compromise my beliefs. It was just that Peter and I had slightly different opinions on what constituted politics. I wanted to bring in more sociopolitical issues, appeal to a younger audience, bring them all to the table.

And I finally figured out how to merge the two so we could both be happy.

I stood outside his office at 9:50 a.m., going over my pitch once more in my head. He wasn't there yet, of course, but I wanted to be ready and waiting for him when he walked in. It was that important. I tapped my leopard print, sling-back kitten heels on the floor while I bided my time and contemplated all the different ways the conversation could go. Peter was a reasonable man, but he was also very stuck in his ways, something I'd have to be sure to combat strategically in our discussion. I shifted in my heels to distract myself and continued waiting.

By the time Peter walked up, I was on pins and needles, and practically jumped him upon his arrival.

"Hey, Reagan, ready for the day, I see?" he asked, glancing down at his watch.

I chuckled awkwardly. "I guess so. I just realized I had some more ideas I wanted to talk through with you if you have time."

"Sure, come on in," he said, stepping inside and proceeding with his morning routine. I'd ambushed Peter so many times at this point, I could recount his steps play by play with my eyes closed: he places his coffee cup on the edge of his desk, shimmies out of his coat, puts it on the coat hanger, walks around to the back side of his desk, sits his briefcase on the floor just off to the right corner of the office, reaches around to get his coffee again and finally, takes a seat in his chair. He does all of this without saying a word, and I oblige, too, not wanting to interrupt him but also to observe. He never looked bored with his routine, I realized. It was who he was and what he liked. And all of a sudden, I had a better understanding of why he was so resistant to my changes.

To Peter, change was opposite from him, and it made sense until now because I was also a creature of habit. My attempts to shake up our content the past few months probably felt like an attack on him, and not what it actually was—an attack on my previous belief in the status quo.

I knew then that I needed to frame my first idea perfectly or he would flip.

"Okay, Reagan. Talk to me. What did you have in mind?" he asked after taking a sip of his coffee.

"So last night I'm home, scrolling through social media, and I had a genius idea I think you'll love." I walked over to the seats in front of his desk and sat down as well.

"I'm intrigued."

"What if I reached out to some female politicians and got them to tell me who they have their eye on in pop culture at the moment? And then did the same with a few women who are making a name for themselves outside Capitol Hill? Then give them a chance to conduct five-to-ten-minute interviews with the women they mentioned, covering the important topics happening each month we do it. I'm talking everyone from Representatives Maxine Waters and Alexandria Ocasio-Cortez to Senator Kirsten Gillibrand and Representative Rashida Tlaib. This way we're staying true to the people who want their Beltway politics, while appealing to a younger online magazine audience." I sat up on the edge of the chair, trying to both contain my excitement but also convey just enough of it that Peter understood I wasn't presenting him with a fly-by-night idea.

I continued, "Can you imagine how dope it would be to read an interview by Elizabeth Warren with Megan Thee Stallion on the cost of college and student loan debt? Now, I have no idea if Senator Warren even knows Megan exists, but if she did, that would be perfect! The no-nonsense rapper who is blowing up right now and also happens to still be in college, obtaining her degree, sitting down with one of the more famous female advocates for student loan relief and higher education. You thought my last piece was gold? This kind of series would be groundbreaking, Peter."

After I'd finished my pitch, I looked at him and held my breath while I tried to read his reaction and get a sense of what he was thinking. He did not make it easy for me, sitting stoically in front of me an entire minute before speaking. And when he finally did, he hemmed and hawed so much at first, I had a nagging feeling I wouldn't like what he wanted to say.

"Reagan, I appreciate your enthusiasm. Really, I do. But this still sounds too kitschy for me. Elizabeth Warren and a gangster rapper? What makes you think a middle-aged white woman in northern Virginia wants to read that?"

"First, she's not a gangster rapper. Jesus, Peter,

seriously? And second, I think the beauty of the idea is that the middle-aged white woman in Virginia will want to read it. You know why? Because her daughters will read it and comment about it and post it on their social media, and that mom wants to know everything her daughter does. But so will the hip-hop blogs and the students currently in college dreading the debt ahead of them six months after they graduate and the women in their thirties poised right between both of these generations—too young to have gone to college for fifty dollars like Warren did, too old to benefit from the information most people know now about predatory lending, but still young enough to listen to Megan in their earphones while they are out conducting grown woman business. This is a win/win. No one could say we're being too light, but it also gets those new investors the increase in eyes and clicks they want."

"I understand, Reagan, but I just don't think this is the proper venue for it. Three fourths of the people you named are not our core audience, and I think we risk alienating them by going this rogue so quickly."

"Okay," I said, leaning back into the chair. "Do you want to hear any of the other ideas I had?"

"Please. Yes." He rubbed his forehead and watched me as I gathered myself again in the chair, feeling defeated, but hoping I could take one more crack at finding a good balance in what we both wanted for the new vertical.

"Black female mayors," I started. "Latoya Cantrell

in New Orleans. Keisha Lance Bottoms in Atlanta. Lori Lightfoot in Chicago. And DC's very own, Muriel Bowser. Are they the new Black quarterbacks? And what are the challenges both face to being viewed as quarterback/mayor first before their identities?"

"No," he replied, not even allowing me the chance to finish. "What is the disconnect we're having here, Reagan?"

"I'm wondering the same thing, to be honest," I said, stunned at his candor. "You told me you trusted me and that this was my opportunity to have my voice heard."

"I did—" He stopped himself before continuing. "I do. But that trust was based on the kind of stories you've produced for us the past four years. These are...different, to say the least. I don't understand what's wrong with the ideas you sent me yesterday. Those were great!"

"They were good, but they were also stories that I knew fit your vision. Not mine. They don't challenge me or push me beyond anything I've done since I got here."

"That's not true. You were just praising me for giving you the chance to do more stories focused on women because that wasn't always the case. How easily you forget having to go to those White House briefings and simply regurgitate whatever news they wanted to give us that day. I'm not the bad guy here."

"Peter, I would never say you're a bad guy. Ever. I just think we are not on the same page about what this vertical can be and the impact it can have. I'm not saying everything I think of will be perfect, but you're not even giving the ideas that aren't the same cookie-cutter ones we are known for a chance."

"You're right, I'm not. But it's because I know what works here."

"Your vision, yes?"

"Let's not forget the success you've had executing my vision." He was definitely growing annoyed with me the longer we kept discussing the issue, but he was not alone.

"Then why offer it to me? Why say the vertical was mine?" I asked on the verge of tears but holding them back.

"Because I thought you got it. I thought you understood what we're doing here. Maybe I was wrong." He spoke with a low voice as he stared me down, very clear on who held the power in our relationship and not needing to raise his voice to get his point across.

"I do get it, Peter," I replied. "But maybe it's not enough for me anymore." I looked across the desk at the man who'd given me my biggest breaks in journalism thus far, the man who'd put my articles on the homepage when he didn't have to, who'd been generous enough to offer me a promotion and wait two months for my response, but he was also the man holding me back, and I couldn't let him or my fears do it anymore.

"I quit," I said quietly. "I'll pack my things up and be out this afternoon."

"Reagan, you don't have to do that. You presented

me a great proposal yesterday. Let's just take some time and focus on that, and maybe these other ideas can come about later."

"I appreciate you, Peter. I really do. But I can't wait anymore. I didn't know that until this conversation, but I just can't."

Seven hours later Rebecca, Robin, Jennifer and Christine were all at my front door, knocking on it incessantly while I walked from my bedroom, through the living room, into the foyer, and until I actually, physically, opened the door.

"Oh, my God, y'all. I was in bed. You didn't have to knock the whole time."

"Please. Be happy we didn't start doing the Total 'No One Else' beat on your door. We're not playing with you," Robin said as she walked past me.

"Ten more seconds and we would have," added Christine.

"Well, I am glad you did not. The unrhythmic knocks were more than enough. Trust."

"What song are we talking about again?" asked Rebecca, prompting Robin and Christine to burst out laughing as they slid their shoes off in the hallway.

"Oh, Becs," said Jennifer, throwing an arm around her shoulder. "We'll have to school you on '90s R&B another day."

She turned to me before continuing. "Today we're here to celebrate Rae finally quitting her job and checking off the second risk on her list."

"I love you guys for being here, but I wouldn't necessarily call this a celebration," I said, walking behind them as we all moved to the living room. "In fact, I'm pretty sure I might have just made the dumbest decision of my life." I plopped down dramatically onto my chaise as the other girls stared at me with equal parts concern and amusement.

"We thought you might be feeling this way, which is why we all came by to remind you how brave you were today."

"I don't feel brave. I think if I learned anything from Luke—"

"Ew, please do not bring his name up," Jennifer interrupted.

"Seriously, he may have been ridiculously sexy, but he was also obviously an idiot. So let's not talk about what you think you learned from him, okay?" Robin added.

"I just mean that there are consequences to these risks," I said with a sigh. "Sure, in that moment it was exhilarating and exciting standing up for myself. But now I'm like, 'Uhhh you don't have a backup job, Rae!' Who quits a job without a job?"

"You!" they all shouted in unison.

I couldn't help but laugh. "Yeah, I guess me. *Ay dios mio!*"

"No, no, no. Don't bring my people into this. *Hablas inglés mientras dudas,*" Christine said, chastising me.

"Bleh." I wanted to throw a tantrum, but I knew

they weren't about to let me do so, at least not while they were there. "Okay, fine. You're all here now, so what's the plan?"

"Oh, I'm glad you finally asked," Rebecca said with a smile. She bent down and picked up the big bag she'd brought with her while Jennifer leaped to her feet and headed toward my kitchen. "You can't celebrate without champagne!" she exclaimed, pulling out four bottles of bubbly from what had initially looked like a shopping bag.

"And…" Jennifer added as she strutted back into the living room with five of my champagne glasses in her hand.

"You definitely can't celebrate without shoes." Robin winked at me as she pulled out a box from the other shopping bag that they brought with them. I looked back at her curiously as she handed me the box. As I gingerly opened it, I heard Rebecca popping open one of the bottles and begin pouring champagne into the glasses. In my lap was a pair of Sophia Webster chocolate satin sandals with brown, tan and crystal floral appliques adorning the straps that crossed your toes.

The very shoes I'd shown Robin and Jennifer months ago when they pressed me about the risk list.

"Oh. My. God," I said in shock. "What did you all do?"

"We got you some shoes, silly," Christine replied.

"Well, yeah. I see that, but—"

"No buts," Robin interjected. "You deserve these.

And it helps that we got them the week after you showed them to us."

"Wait, what?" I was blown away. *What did I ever do to deserve these girls?* I thought. In fact, I didn't deserve them, these shoes, or the first pair I bought as a reward on the risk list. But if they thought I did—with all the ways they showed up as dynamic, awesome, boss-ass friends—then maybe I could start to believe them.

"We knew you would get to this point, eventually," Robin continued. "To be honest, we thought you'd quit *and* have a new job, so we wanted to be ready. When you showed us those heels, Jennifer and I instantly decided they were going to come from us. And then we couldn't leave Christine and Rebecca out."

"I thought I'd have a new job before quitting, too," I laughed.

"But that's okay. Because, honestly, this took so much more courage. And I, for one, am in awe of what you did today." Robin raised her glass and pointed to the rest of the girls to get them to do the same.

"Absolutely," Jennifer shouted.

"Sabes cómo me siento," said Christine.

"I'm going to miss seeing you at work every day, but I couldn't be prouder," Rebecca said.

It took everything in me to stop from crying. Instead, I raised my glass to meet theirs and cleared my throat before speaking. "I love you girls, for real."

"We know," they replied in unison, laughing, as we all took big gulps of our drinks.

"Now can we talk about how this one spent all day yesterday avoiding me because she knew accepting that promotion was wrong to begin with?" Rebecca asked, pointing toward me.

"Wow, this is what we're doing?"

"Oh, yes, this is definitely what we're doing." She nudged me in my side and took another sip of her drink.

"If I'm being fully honest, I wasn't just avoiding you because of the promotion. I also didn't want to talk about Luke."

"Right. I learned that, too, after meeting up with the girls," she said with a little bit of annoyance in her voice that turned back to folly quickly. "But you all should have seen her. Just typing away like a mad woman. No, better yet, like that gif of the cat on the laptop."

"OMG, the one where the cat's going crazy and just beating the keyboard with his hands all fast?" Jennifer asked.

"That exact one."

"You are wild for that," Robin said, chiming in.

I shrugged and laughed off their jokes. "It was an act of preservation," I admitted. "You see how she's being now. Just think about how it would have been in the office."

"Mmm, she does make a good point," said Christine.

As they were talking and debating the merits of my avoiding Rebecca's glares at work, I heard my phone begin vibrating. I pressed the screen to see who it might be and saw a familiar name: Jake Saunders. *Damn*.

I looked up to see if anyone else noticed his name and saw Robin giving me a knowing look. "Please don't say anything," I mouthed.

"I won't," she responded, picking up her phone as she kept her eyes on me.

Is that a thing again? she asked over text. I reached for my phone once more so I could reply without anyone discovering this conversation, too.

Absolutely not.

Then why is he calling you?

That's a great question. I have no clue.

Hmm. I think I know.

Do you?

Yeah, he got the bat signal. You know how guys are. Somehow they are immediately aware as soon as you either start dating someone or you break up.

I need him to lose my signal and my number.

I tried to stop myself from laughing but was having a hard time as Robin and I continued texting in the middle of the living room with everyone else unaware. I knew I wouldn't be able to keep going much longer without alerting the rest of the group, especially with Robin—of all people—texting about bat signals. I placed my phone back on the coffee table and turned it upside down.

"Anyone need any more champagne?" I asked while popping another bottle.

"Ohh! Someone's finally ready to celebrate?" Rebecca asked.

"Might as well," I replied and poured myself another glass.

Chapter Twelve

Alone at home a few days later, I found myself staring at those Sophia Webster heels again. They were so beautiful, and I loved the way the chocolate satin complemented my skin tone. It was as if we were made to be together, with the way the colors and jewels popped when on my feet. But as much as the girls tried to convince me that I deserved them, I couldn't shake the feeling it was simply a really pretty pity gift. After all, just two days before then, I was doing the exact opposite of the risk list: accepting the promotion because it felt like a safer bet.

Had I really been that brave or just so fed up that quitting became the only option?

I honestly didn't know the answer. But one thing I did know was that even if I didn't truly earn those heels now, I could make damn sure I deserved them soon enough. And the best way I knew how to do that was to type out what I wanted in my next job and commit to myself that no matter what, I wouldn't settle for less. I grabbed my laptop from my desk and began typing:

- *Must be a job that allows me to champion women across age groups, race, ethnicities, sexuality and cultures.*
- *Must come with a level of autonomy, not a promise of it to come.*
- *Must allow for a broader definition of politics that speaks to the sociopolitical ways we are affected in our daily lives by the policies enacted throughout the country.*
- *Supportive, non-micromanaging supervisor.*
- *At least $10K more than what I was making at my last job.*

I looked over my notes again. Now, this was a list I could truly get behind. I sat for a beat to consider if I was forgetting anything before beginning my job search again. I wanted to go into it this time with more intention than when Robin, Jennifer and I were looking. Maybe I could avoid the cat blog and technical writer job descriptions.

After adding three more items to the list, I felt satisfied. It wasn't going to be an easy task, but it was one I was willing to take on, for the love of those chocolate sandals. Just then, I heard my phone vibrating.

"Hello?" I answered, always sort of stunned when someone picked up the phone and actually called me.

"Buenos días, querida."

"Hi, Mama Vasquez, what's wrong?" I could hear in her voice she'd been crying.

"Christine was rushed to the hospital again."

"Oh, no. Same one as before?"

"Si, mija. Dominic is there now, *pero* I can't get a flight until this evening."

"I'm leaving now. I should get there in fifteen-twenty minutes. Don't worry, we got her."

"Gracias, mija. No puedo tomar un vuelo hasta noche."

I hurriedly threw on some jeans to go with my T-shirt, pulled out my slide-on mules to make putting my shoes on at the door go faster, grabbed my coat from my closet and began calling my rideshare car before even stepping out my front door. Time was of the essence, and I wanted to be outside as soon as it arrived so I could jump in and get to the hospital as soon as possible.

Three minutes later I was in the backseat of the car as we drove through the streets of DC. Christine had only been out of the hospital two and a half months this time around, which was certainly not a good sign for her health. Scared and anxious to get to her, I tried closing my eyes for the rest of the ride to steady myself. I knew I'd have to be strong when I got there, but right now everything just hurt.

It took us twenty minutes in traffic to arrive and another five for me to race through the hospital to get to the intensive care unit, explain that I was basically family and then get to her room door. Dominic was seated next to her as she lay still trying to breathe through a hundred million tubes and wires. I walked in and put on my best brave face.

"Christine Vasquez, what are we doing back here?" I asked with a forced small smile. "I believe we made a pact of no hospital visits this year. Do you know what a pact is, *mana*?"

"Chica," she said with a weak voice. "It doesn't look like it, but I did try."

"Hmph. Seems to me like March isn't much of a try."

She laughed as much as she could before beginning to cough and then starting to cry.

"No, no, no, I'm sorry," I said, rushing to her side. "It was too much. I shouldn't have gone that far."

"It was perfect. I just hate being back here again."

"I know, honey. I know." I took her hand in mine and held it. "But you are in the best place to feel better. What happened, by the way?"

I turned back to Dominic, looking to him to help explain since I could see she was straining to talk.

"We were at her place, and she started coughing up blood. We thought maybe it was just a side effect of one of the medicines or she had overdone things, but as I was walking her to her room so she could lie down, she almost passed out in my arms. I knew then I had to call 911."

"Oh, my God, friend." I looked back at Christine and saw the fear in her eyes. She was worried about this one, which made me that much more concerned. "So what are the doctors saying?"

"They need to run a bunch of tests and see what's going on," Dominic replied. He sounded so exhausted and defeated as he explained the details to me. "Honestly, Rae, it feels like dèjá vu all over again."

"I can understand that, Dominic. Do you feel that way, too, Chrissy?"

"I do, Reagan. I really do." Tears streamed down her face as she held my hand tightly.

"Then it's a good thing I'm here to remind you both that things have looked bleak before, and you made it through, because you are a warrior. You may not feel that way at this very moment, but the fight you have inside you has kept you alive all this time, and that's not stopping. And the people who love you, both of you, will be here to pick up that fight if you don't feel you have the strength to do it right now." It was all I could do to keep it together, but I looked at her and then him to make sure they understood me clearly.

Squeezing Christine's hand, I turned back to her and invoked a *Game of Thrones* expression that we'd taken on as our own over the years. "What do we say to the god of Death?" I asked.

"Not today."

"Exactly. Not today."

"Thank you, Reagan," Dominic said.

"Don't mention it… I should step out for a second to make sure your mom called the girls. I know she was planning to, but she was really flustered when she called me, so who knows."

"Oh, please check, Reagan. I would hate—"

"Ah, not another word. I'll be back," I said, finally letting her hand go. I definitely did want to check to see if the girls were on their way, but it was also the perfect excuse to leave the room before I started crying in front of her. The last thing she needed to see was me losing it, but I was struggling to hold back my tears each time she squeezed my hand or broke down herself.

I opened her room door and stepped out into the cold, sterile hallway. It was something about the crisp whiteness of hospital hallways and the stillness in the atmosphere that always did me in. They just felt so impersonal and isolating for a place meant to be a spot where people went for healing. I was two steps down the hallway when I looked up and saw Jake turn the corner, recognize me and come running to my aid.

He was inches away from me when I fell into his arms and began crying. All the anger I'd felt toward him, the hurt he caused me, the stupid ways he'd played me…they all meant nothing in this moment. He was here when I needed him the most. And I could no longer hold my tears back as he stood without a word and let me soak his shirt with sobs for minutes, only occasionally rubbing my hair to bring me comfort.

"Maybe we should go for a walk," he finally said.

"A walk sounds good."

"Wait, what are you doing here?" I asked once I had a moment to calm down. We'd walked to Jake's car to get some privacy while I tried drying up my tears, but the peace and quiet away from the hospital walls also brought me back to reality. It certainly didn't help that Jake had the kind of car a man gets when he has no intention of having obligations any time soon: a two-seater, silver Jaguar F-TYPE. It was gorgeous on the outside, intimate inside and was also a stark reminder of the reason we broke up in the first place.

"Christine's mom called me. I assume she was just going through the numbers she had of her friends, and I was still on the list."

"Oh."

I guess I'd forgotten that Mama Vasquez had Jake's number from when we were in college. And that we hadn't exactly updated her to let her know he shouldn't still be on the call list of people to inform if something went wrong.

"And so you came all the way from New York?"

"Actually, no. I was in town already for work. It's why I called you the other night as well. Was hoping we could talk after all these years. But then when Chrissy's mom called, I just figured it was fate I was here, and so I should come."

"You definitely came around that corner just as I needed you to," I admitted with a sigh. "I'm sorry about that, by the way. I just... I couldn't cry in there and then I saw you and—"

"Hey, you don't have to apologize for that. I'm—I don't want to say glad but—grateful I was there when you needed someone."

"Thank you. I don't want to make this about me, though. She's the one in there fighting for her life. I was simply trying to encourage her to keep doing so because... I'm... I'm just not ready to lose my friend." I held back more tears that were aching to flow down my cheeks.

"And it's okay to feel that," he said, lifting my head so we were eye to eye. "It's okay to not be everyone's strength all the time. That's all I'm saying."

"Yeah, I hear you."

"I don't think you do, but that's okay, too. Just know you don't have to be strong with me. I can take your tears and your questions."

And there it was: Jake's habit of saying the perfect thing at the right time. It had always been a hallmark of his, but since we hadn't spoken in so long, I'd somehow forgotten how comforting he could be. Which meant I was all at once calm and also fighting not to run out of his car as fast as I could to get away from him and his charm.

"Um, so back to why you called me the other day," I said, trying to move on to a different conversation. "I feel like a jerk now for not answering, but I was sort of in the middle of something."

"You must have been in the middle of something for four years," he said with a slight chuckle.

"Okay, don't act like you've been calling me non-stop and I just haven't answered."

"I've called you a few times and you never answered. Maybe not nonstop but enough for me to get the hint you didn't want to hear from me."

"What changed this time? Why call now, just because you were in town?"

"No, I'm in DC a lot lately actually. I don't know, I think maybe I wanted to try my luck again. See if you believed me this time when I told you that I was sorry for not choosing you before and that I miss you."

I fought back tears again while I listened to him, my heart swelling from the words I'd so desperately wanted to hear years before.

"The truth is I miss my best friend, Reagan, and my partner, the woman I always hoped I'd spend the rest of my life with. And, I don't know, I just thought I'd try calling you again."

The silence between us was still and felt like it would never end, but I had nothing to say to break it. My brain was too full replaying Jake's words to formulate my own as we sat there staring at each other. A tear I couldn't catch trickled down my cheek as I thought about this being the first time that he apologized for how he'd hurt me senior year and how badly I'd needed to hear that from him. Coupling his apology with also calling me the woman he'd hoped to spend the rest of his life with in the very same breath was almost too much for me to handle.

Jake leaned closer to me and wiped the tear off my face. "I told you I can handle your tears, remember? You don't have to hold anything back from me."

And with that, he kissed my forehead, his lips lightly pressing against my skin as I cried softly underneath him. Within seconds I angled my face upward and his lips moved down to mine, kissing me deeply and with urgency like his life depended on it. A moan escaped from my mouth as pleasure shot down my spine, and his right hand grabbed a handful of my hair, pulling me closer to him.

"I missed this, too," he said breathlessly. "I could have kissed you all night after Lance and Candice's wedding."

Ugh. The wedding.

Hearing those words sent shivers through my body, and I pulled back from him, suddenly wishing his car allowed for more room between us. How could I have forgotten the last time we were kissing had led to me realizing I still loved him when all he was looking for was a wedding fling with an ex?

"Damn, I shouldn't have said that." Jake leaned

back against his window after seeing the hurt in my face, putting even more space in between us.

"I don't look at that time between us fondly," I admitted.

"I know you don't. I do, though," he said with a sigh. "At least part of it. I thought we had a really great night, Rae, and then I woke up the next morning and you were gone. No note, no explanation."

"You don't think I had a reason to leave?"

"I think you probably saw some texts on my phone and jumped to conclusions."

"Oh, I saw them, yes. And it didn't take much of a jump, trust me."

"Are you kidding me? We're adults. You could have asked me about it. Or, here's an idea, not been snooping in my phone in the first place."

"I wasn't!" I could feel myself getting heated. No way was he going to try to turn this argument on to me. "Your boys were blowing you up the whole time we were in bed, and I ignored it until I couldn't take it anymore. What started as me trying to silence your phone turned into me seeing just how you felt about me, learning about your *girlfriend* and realizing how much I'd been played."

"For the record, Shannon was not my girlfriend at the time. If you'd talked to me, I could have told you that she and I broke up because I realized I was still in love with you. But you didn't give me that chance. The fact is the only person who got played that night was me." Jake sat up straight and folded his arms as he sought to get his point across. He'd clearly lost his lovey-dovey feelings from moments ago as well. "Because it was once again you deciding on a story about us and allowing every little thing to fuel that belief."

"Every little thing?" I was incensed. "I don't call those texts some little thing, even *if* the Shannon part wasn't true. The rest of the texts were proof enough I was right not to trust you, that all you'd wanted from me—"

"Was what? Sex?" he asked, interrupting me. "C'mon, Reagan, you think I'm that hard up for sex I'd trick a woman I loved for a one-night stand? What the hell?"

"I don't know, Jake. I just know what I saw."

"Exactly. You let one thing you saw negate everything I'd been telling you all night. Just like you let one moment between us, when I was young and dumb and not knowing what to do with a relationship at twenty-one, define everything about us. But I shouldn't be surprised. That's what you do. You've never fully trusted that I loved you. You've never trusted…me."

"I did trust you at one point. And you broke my heart." My eyes swelled up with tears again as my voice cracked. I wasn't sure if they were angry tears, sad ones, or some combination of both, but I knew I had to fight them at all costs. "You were my best friend. You knew it all, how scared I was to be played again after Matthew, how my parents' divorce messed me up, and still—"

"So I couldn't be scared, too? Is that what you're saying?"

"No, I'm saying you could have been scared and still decided we were better off figuring it out together. You could have still chosen me, and you didn't."

"I'm trying to now." His voice lowered as he calmed himself and slumped down in his seat, exhausted.

"It's too late, Jake. I can't take the chance of being disappointed again right now, especially not by you. It would hurt too much, and I can't handle that between everything with Christine and…" I stopped myself before continuing, realizing I hadn't told him about quitting my job just four days earlier or my breakup with Luke. He wouldn't understand the pressure I was feeling from the work decision alone, and I didn't want to get into either of them with him while he was basically telling me I was the reason we never worked out. *Hadn't this all started as an apology from him?* That seemed long gone.

"And what, Reagan? Please, tell me what's the excuse now," he said, the frustration spewing from his mouth.

"And nothing," I lied. "I just want to be off this merry-go-round. You should probably go back home where you don't have to worry about people disregarding your feelings, as you said, and creating stories that paint you in a bad light."

"And I guess you'll go back to that guy you've been seeing."

"Wow, so is that what all this was about? You heard I was seeing someone and that's the real reason you called."

"Here we go with the stories again. I just sat here and told you why I called and what I wanted, but you still don't believe me." He threw up his hands in defeat. "I can't do anything about that."

"You're right. I don't believe you. And I wish you'd never come today." I opened my passenger door and began climbing out of the car. "Please don't call me again."

"Bet."

I heard his last word before slamming the door shut and turning to go back to the hospital. This was definitely goodbye. That much was clear. Looking down at my shoes, I realized just how much I'd still been subconsciously hoping for something that brought us back together, that made me believe in him again, because for some reason I still loved him. But just like the mules I had on, I couldn't count on him when things got rough. They were easy to put on when needed, but ever try running in shoes with no back to them? That was how I felt every time I thought about being with Jake again; like whatever benefits might come, the danger was too much to risk it. The more I looked at the shoes, the more I felt the tears start to well up inside me once again.

I was barely feet away from his car before I heard him speed off. *Typical. And Rebecca always chided me for being the one to run away.* Now furious on top of my hurt, I walked back into the hospital and texted Robin and Jennifer to see if they'd heard from Mama Vasquez. In all the chaos, I realized I hadn't reached out to them or Rebecca yet, but in that moment I desperately needed a distraction from what I'd just gone through. Still, the last thing I could stomach was three individual phone calls then so text would have to suffice.

Hey girls, did you hear from Mama Vasquez? I typed.

Yeah, I'm on my way now, Jennifer wrote back.

Two minutes later Robin chimed in. Same.

Okay, good. I'm here now. See you soon.

Next, I texted Rebecca:

Hey Becs, Chrissy was rushed to the hospital today. She's stable and I'm here with her now, but they are running a bunch of tests. Just wanted to let you know.

Thanks, Rae. I'm so sorry to hear that. Please give her my love and let me know when it'll be appropriate to come visit.

Will do. Thanks, Becs.

* * *

Back in Christine's room, I sat down next to Dominic as we both quietly watched her sleep. Even with all the tubes connected to her, she looked peaceful and without pain. I only wished she could feel that peace when she was awake and not tied to a hospital bed by machines both monitoring her and working to keep her alive.

"Everything okay?" he asked.

"Yeah, I just needed a breather earlier, but I'm good now. Found out Robin and Jennifer will be here soon, too."

"She may not even know they are here, you know. She's pretty worn out."

"Doesn't matter, Dominic. They'll know," I said, reaching for his hand. "And you'll know, too. We are here for you as much as we are for her."

"I appreciate it," he said. I could tell he really meant it, but also saw that he was just as exhausted as Christine.

"How about I go wait in the visitors' lounge until they get here? That way I can update them on everything before they come in the room, and you can get some rest while she sleeps."

"You sure you're okay with that?"

"Yeah, very. I am happy to do it."

"Thanks, Reagan. That would be great. I can't wait until Mama Vasquez gets here to help, but I think I *could* use a few minutes of resting my eyes. It was a really hard day."

"I bet. Just text me if you need anything, okay?"

"Will do."

I walked back out of Christine's room and put my earphones in to drown out my thoughts and the white noise hum of the hospital. Music was what I needed in that moment, and I knew just the song. I'd be on my fifth replay of Jhené Aiko's "None of Your Concern" by the time Robin and Jennifer came into the visitors' lounge and caught me lip synching the most important lyric, my head to the sky, feeling every single word to the core.

Like Jhené, I was completely over the idea that some guy could question me when he was the one who left.

Chapter Thirteen

"Dammit!"

I dropped my charcoal-gray work bag in my hallway in complete frustration of how my latest interview had gone, walked into my living room, kicked off my shoes and sank into my couch like a woman with the weight of the world on her shoulders. I was supposed to be coming home and changing really quickly so I could go see Christine in the hospital again, but first I needed a chance to sit and take a deep breath. I looked down at my cobalt blue Jessica Simpson pumps adorned with a sky blue bow at the tip of the shoe and contemplated pitching them straight out my window. Sure, it wasn't their fault I'd just been on yet another disappointing interview, but in that moment they were the symbol of everything that had gone wrong in the month that passed since quitting my job.

Christine was still in the hospital. After seven interviews, I was no closer to finding a new job, and my savings was steadily dwindling down. And oh, I couldn't stop replaying that horrible fight between me and Jake, so my dating life had basically dried up, too. April was turning out to be a really big bust.

Having breathed long enough on my couch, I stood up to pour myself a glass of wine and then walked to my bedroom to change clothes. Pulling out a pair of jeans and a T-shirt, I went over in my head the course of the interview, just to see what I could have possibly done differently. It was a practice I'd started after the first interview to make sure I did my part to be better at each one, but this one felt different the more I thought about it. It started out fine enough. That is until the two men interviewing me started speaking about the real duties of the job, which were quite different than what I read in the job description and compared to my list of what I wanted in my next job.

One guy sat behind a chrome desk, his left leg casually placed over his right and lightly grazing the desk while he leaned back with his hands behind his head. The other, possibly meant to be the formal bad cop of the two, sat in a chair next to me with a checkered blue-and-white shirt, tie to match and sleeves that were rolled up perfectly halfway up his arms.

As I sat there stunned, sitting across from them in

an office decorated in what could only be described as medical office chic, I quickly learned that my impressions of what they were offering—a chance to write about complex women's issues for a popular national website—were very off. In fact, what they were really looking for was a woman to write features that were all about men. This triggered a very visceral and unprofessional reaction from me, but one that made me proud of myself just as much as I was upset with the circumstances.

"You see, Reagan, we've noticed that our webpage hits grow exponentially when the column focuses on content centered around relationships and dating—"

"Right," interjected the other editor, his matching checkered tie all of a sudden commanding my attention. "Kind of like *Cosmopolitan* magazine meets Carrie from *Sex and the City*. You girls like that kind of stuff, yes?"

"Uhhh, yeah, I enjoy both *Cosmo* and *Sex and the City*," I started, trying not to focus too much on his usage of girls vs. women. "But I was under the impression this column would focus on a range of *women's* issues, and that I'd have the opportunity to cover everything from relationship concerns to healthcare to sports, reproductive rights, politics and everything in between?"

"Well, it *was* that, but we just don't think it's in the website's best interest to continue that sort of column. That's not what girls want to read. They want to read things like *Fifty ways to please my man*—"

"Oh, and *How to tell if he really likes me*," interjected the second editor again.

"Wow." I was practically speechless and couldn't believe these two men were trying to tell me, a woman, what women wanted to read.

"Do you not agree?" the first editor asked, looking at me with his forehead beginning to crease.

I sat there for a beat, trying to decide just how honest I should be in that moment. The composed, young and Black professional in me wanted to be the bigger person, put on my best fake smile and politely leave when the time was right. But the longer I sat there, the more I realized I wouldn't be able to hold much of my contempt in, and I didn't leave my comfy job with Peter to put up with this crap from two tone-deaf men who had reduced a groundbreaking women's magazine and TV series to simply being about what men wanted from women. Then to insist on calling us *girls* after I corrected them and imply that we wouldn't want to read compelling content that spoke to us as more than just objects for men to ogle? My blood was literally boiling.

"Hmm. I guess it depends on your target audience," I said, hedging my words at first. "I see your target audience as independent, fiery, yet intelligent women between twenty-five and forty-four, who, sure, may want to discuss fun things like dating and marriage, but also want to delve into the serious issues that concern them. Especially in this time, I think women are looking for more. I know I am."

The second editor sat back in his seat and made awkward eye contact with the one behind the desk. I guess it was their time to be speechless.

"And frankly," I continued, emboldened. "I don't think any woman reading *my* work would like to be put into one neat little box that focuses only on what men want from women. That's too simple and far too one-dimensional. You'll notice that even *Cosmo*, to use your example, not only has a bustling money and career section, but also ones on politics, health and fitness and college in addition to their famed sex and relationships posts. That's because they understand women want to read about more than just men, and it's worked out really well for them. *Teen Vogue*'s profile rose specifically because of the ways they've connected with their audience on sociopolitical issues they care about in addition to fashion. This just seems like really outdated thinking to me."

"Well," said the first editor, "we're not looking for some 'Me Too' writer here, so—"

The second editor interrupted. "I guess it's safe to say this probably isn't the job for you, missy."

Damn. And he hit me with the universal blow-off missy *moniker. Oh, well.* I knew as soon as I said my last statement that I wouldn't be getting the job, but I also knew I'd regret it if I hadn't. I wanted to protest further that it was a lazy and poor characterization to just lump anything not about relationships as a part of the "Me Too" movement, but that also it was ironic they were disparaging it and highlighting the reasons for it at the same time. But sadly, it just felt like it would be a waste of my time. Instead, I opted to make a gracious exit before I said anything else that might get me thrown out of the building.

"Thank you for your time, gentlemen," I said while placing my résumé into my portfolio. "I really appreciate the opportunity I've had to speak with you."

I stood up and shook both of their hands, looking them straight in their eyes to show I held no regrets for standing up for what I believed in during the interview. Even if my insides were screaming, "Retreat! Take it back! Hurry!"

"Have a wonderful afternoon," I said before turning on my heels to walk out of the office.

"Same to you, Ms. Doucet," said the first editor.

"I'm really sorry we couldn't make this work," the second one offered as well.

And to be honest, I was, too. Before they switched it up on me, I'd gone into that interview really excited about the opportunity and hopeful that this was the one that made quitting my job worth it. So while I was proud of myself for not settling, this was yet another blow to the armor I'd been carrying to shield me from the thing I was desperately trying not to feel: that I was a failure.

I pulled a pair of white-and-gold sandals out of my closet, buckled them around my ankles and grabbed my bag back from the hallway on my way out to the Metro train station. I'd been home less than twenty minutes, but I knew if I stayed any longer, I'd just want to sink into my couch and will everything to disappear. Better to at least go spend some time with Christine; she needed the company, and I needed to hear her raucous laugh.

"Hey, boo," I said, walking into Christine's new room in the step-down unit. In the past week she'd been transferred there as her doctors felt she needed less intensive care. While that was an improvement, we were still very worried that they didn't think she was healthy enough to go home or even just a general medical ward. When I walked in this time, however, she had a different glow about her.

"Hola, mana. Cómo tú ta?"

"I'm all right," I said with a sigh. "Just happy to see you sitting up. You look a little livelier today."

"You know, when the good days come, I try to enjoy them as much as I can. And today has been a good one so far. I even started catching up on some podcasts earlier today."

"That's great, Chrissy. I'm so happy to hear that." I took my seat and moved it closer to her bed like always before sitting. I understood why the chairs were positioned away from the beds so they didn't block any of the doctors or nurses when they needed to come in to see a patient, but I hated how far away from her I felt when I kept the chair where it was supposed to be. I was there to visit her, after all, not look at her from behind a glass window.

"Are you, *mana*? You seem not really happy at all, actually."

Leave it to Chrissy. Somehow, she always knew.

"You have a lot going on, Chrissy. You definitely don't need to hear about my little guitar woes."

"Girl, please. Trying not to die does not constitute a lot going on."

"Christine!"

"Lo siento. Pero es verdad," she said, chuckling, giving way to that laugh I'd been missing. It boomed louder than her frail body would ever look like it could make, but it filled the room so gloriously. *This was what I needed.* "Plus, I need someone to talk to me about anything other than my recovery or lack thereof. So go, tell me."

"You make me want to slap you sometimes," I said, laughing back with her. "Anyway, I had another interview today, and it went, in one word, horribly."

"Ay, dios mio. What happened?"

"Basically, I thought I was going in there, ready to become this generation's mixture of Christiane Amanpour, Soledad O'Brien and Danyelle Smith, and they shut that right on *down*," I said, telling her the story of what happened. By the time I'd finished replaying the whole scene, props and all, Christine was barely able to breathe from laughing so hard. Thinking back on it and hearing her get so much joy out of it, I guess it was kind of funny. But I'd still felt so discouraged by it, I explained.

"Oh, pobresita," Christine said, still trying to

catch her breath. "You stood up for what you be-lieved in. You can't fault yourself for that."

"I know. But look where it got me. Still jobless. Still waiting for the perfect opportunity to prove I was right turning down Peter's offer. Stuck in the same place I was a month ago."

"You want to talk about being stuck in the same place for a month?" she asked, pointing around the room and raising her right eyebrow at me.

"Ugh, okay, fair."

"I'm just saying. You're not stuck. You're in tran-sition, and that is not an easy place to be. But you and I both know there's no point in jumping from the pot to the frying pan."

"Oh emmm geee, sometimes I don't know if you're really Latina or secretly country as hell!" I screamed out in laughter.

"What?"

"That's definitely something my mom would say. Or my grandpa. And you know they both have that good old-school Creole country in them."

"Hey, those are smart people! And you know what I mean. There's no point in you leaving someplace you didn't like just to wind up in another place that you like even less."

"No, I get it. Don't move just to move. I just didn't think I'd still be job searching at this point," I said with a sigh. "To be honest, even though I threw out my risk list, I still thought the universe was using it somehow. That I'd get rewarded, and things would fall into place because I—"

"Because you leaped?" she asked, interrupting me.

"*Yes*. Isn't that supposed to mean something?"

"It does. It means you have an even greater chance for falling." Christine repositioned herself in the bed so she could face me more directly. "That's not a bad thing, though, *mana*. It's actually what's beautiful about stepping out of your comfort zone, because without that, you don't ever get the greater chance for soaring, either. I'm learning that in here. Not something I thought I'd learn within these four walls, but I get it now. I used to feel like such a failure every time I ended up in the hospital again—and tomorrow I might go back to feeling like that—but after four years of this, I realize each time is another chance for me to get back up and live out loud again while I still can."

"I don't know, *chica*. I'm just not sure it's worth it for me anymore. You? Yes. And I love that you've found that spark, especially in here," I said, moving my hands to indicate the space in her room as well. "But I'm so tired. I took on this risk list because I thought it would make my life better, and it's only made things worse. Everything I've tried has failed. Maybe safe wasn't so bad after all." I slumped down in my chair and hung my head, afraid to even look at her with my last words.

"Safe was really bad, Rae. It was," she said, leaning closer to me and taking my hand. "And you can't tell me it felt good faking happiness all those years. Doesn't matter if other people looked at you like this super-successful woman living the life if you were so busy playing a role, you don't even know yourself, much less like what you see. But the risk list and this thing that you want to do—write about all the ways women are impacted by what surrounds them and the ways we then impact our surroundings? Those are *absolutely* worth the struggles and the ups and downs. You just can't buy into the myth that it will be easy to strike out and do the scary things, because that's—*una mentira*. If it was easy, everyone would do it, *mana*."

"Yeah," I sighed, still refusing to look at her, ashamed for complaining to her about job searching for a month and being dumped when she'd been fighting for her life at the same time.

"*Mírame*. You've come too far to turn back now, *mana*. I want to see you get this right, and not to make things too depressing, but I don't think I have that much longer to see it." She squeezed my hand as I finally looked back at her, tears welling in my eyes.

"What do you mean?"

"I don't know. I just feel it. The doctors say I'm getting better, but I can tell. I'm dying. And I know that's sad, and it sucks royally, because I'm not ready. But it also kicks my butt into full gear. I can't waste any more time. The last hospital visit made me want to sing more, but now I simply want to *feel* more, touch everything around me, smell the amazing food people cook that I can't eat. I want it all!" Her voice cracked as she spoke, and I could hear her swallow back her tears, which only made me want to grab her and tell her she was wrong, and we could beat this thing once again. Something told me it wasn't what she needed in that moment, though, so I quietly just listened.

"I'm not saying this to guilt trip you," she continued, her voice getting quieter. "*Pero*, I want you to live, *mana*. And not perfectly. *No cautelosa.* Just happy, *bueno.*"

I laid my head on top of her hand and let a single tear finally drop from my eyes. If I could, I would bottle her up and never let her leave my side. Since I couldn't, I tried to take in her scent and her touch as much as I could. "I'm sorry, *mana*," I said, once I finally lifted my head to look at her. "I should be talking about this with anyone else but you. But thank you anyway. *Te quiero mucho.*"

"Because I don't take your mess," she said, flashing a smile again.

"Something like that."

"And I love you, too. The ways you've been there for me over the years, but especially these past four... I can't begin to tell you how much that means to me." Her voice cracked again, and I knew it was officially time to change the subject.

"Okay, so what does living out loud mean this week for you?" I asked.

"First, I have to go on a QVC cleanse this week."

"Wait, what?"

"*Lo sé!* Hear me out. When you're home all day for weeks and weeks, it can really catch up with you. I was on there buying stuff that I seriously have no need for. I thought y'all were going to have to do an intervention or something."

"You know what? I can't with you."

"It was getting ugly, *mana*. The other day I bought some baking contraption. I can't even eat like that. What the hell am I going to do with a baking contraption?"

"I have no idea," I said, bursting out laughing. "But I'm glad you caught yourself before QVC sent you into deep debt."

"Seriously. And I can't explain that to my mom or Dominic. Like, can you lend me some money, Mom? No, not for my medical expenses, for my QVC expenses."

"Bwahahahahaha that would not go over well."

"Not at all."

"All right, *after* the QVC cleanse, then what?" It was her turn to be on the hot seat now.

She thought for a second before answering, and then sat up straight as the idea popped into her head. "Do more of this, I think. I've belly laughed more today than I have in weeks."

"I like that. That's a good one."

"What about you? What is my little Reagan

Doucet going to do when she leaves me this evening?"

"Hmm. You know what I was thinking of? I left my cobalt blue heels in the middle of my living room floor when I came here—"

"Oh, my God, Reagan, no one cares you didn't put your shoes back into the closet!"

"No, that's not what I meant. Now *you* hear me out."

"Okay, okay," she said, throwing her hands up.

"I left them in the middle of the floor because I was upset and feeling like they were just another reminder of my failures. But I want to change that. They are actually the shoes I wore when I didn't settle for less than I deserved. And that's something I know about myself now—when pushed, I can and will push back. For me. I like knowing that. So I want to commemorate them when I get home with a shoe of the day post. Let the people know what they witnessed today. And then, yes, I need to put them where they belong." I winked at her and cracked up at my own joke.

"What am I going to do with you, *chile*?" she asked with an eye roll.

"Love me, of course. And stay on me about stepping out of my comfort zone."

"Lo tienes."

Part 3: There's No Point in Owning Perfect Shoes that Never Leave the Closet

"I like Cinderella; I really do. She has a good work ethic. I appreciate a good, hardworking gal. And she likes shoes. The fairy tale is all about the shoe at the end, and I'm a shoe girl."

—Amy Adams

Chapter Fourteen

"Okay. You can do this. Be confident. Be assured. Be yourself."

I looked at myself in the mirror one last time, straightened out my black pencil dress and slid on my nude semirounded-toe, three-inch pumps from Aldo. It had been a week since my conversation where Christine ran me over the rails and kicked my butt good enough that I went home, found this posting and applied immediately. *SELENE* was a national publication that was only a few years old but seeking to rebrand itself to the modern woman, and the deputy editor was looking for someone with the drive and direction to help them do just that. We'd already spoken on the phone and talked salary, so all that was left was to actually go and meet her for the interview.

Picking up my work bag before I walked out the door, I double-checked to ensure I had my résumé and a formal notebook and pen, took in a deep breath and then finally made my way to the Metro station near my apartment. It was another thirty minutes before I stepped into the building for my interview, and when I did, I felt an energy with me I hadn't had in months. While the glass exterior of the building felt odd in a city not really known for that aesthetic, the marble floors and the mile-high ceiling in the lobby made me feel like you had to have your big-girl panties on to work here. And I wanted something just like that.

I silently shifted my weight on each heel while I waited for Alexandra, the deputy editor, to meet me. I had only found a few photos of her online, but when a tall, brown-skinned woman stepped off the elevator a few minutes later and practically glided toward me, I knew it was her. She reached her hand out to mine and introduced herself.

"You must be Reagan," she said with a smile that seemed completely genuine.

"Yes, I am. And it's so great to meet you."

"Same here. I'm looking forward to our conversation." She motioned toward the conference door to the right of us and walked in ahead of me. Inside was a glass conference table that looked like it easily fit forty or fifty chairs around it. She chose two seats on the corner, so we could sit facing each other without it being uncomfortable. Before I knew it, what

I'd thought would be an interview had turned into a discussion between two women about the viability of women's magazines and the content women wanted to read at the start of a new decade.

"I understand many people feel that printed magazines are a dying business," I said. "But I don't think that's the case. I think if you give people good content, they'll read it in any way that they can. And I also think that we underestimate how much some people love to still turn the pages of their materials. I do. I have a Kindle and a tablet, but I still believe there's nothing like having good content in your hands."

"I agree with you, Reagan. But how would you convince the digital age of women to go out and buy our magazines or subscribe?"

"We've seen certain models work better than others when you talk about incorporating digital media into your world. But one that seems to work best is using the website and social media accounts as opportunities to discuss sidebars of the original content that's given in the magazine. You can even tease the audience with great excerpts online and then make it so that the rest of the content needs to be viewed in the actual magazine. It's all about letting both work together instead of competing with each other for content and audience."

"Basically, it's not about reinventing the wheel—"

"But about understanding your audience and making the wheel work best for you," I said.

"Mmm. Okay. And what kind of content do you think women are clamoring to read?"

"Everything," I blurted out. "I know that sounds generic, but I think far too often we've attempted to box women in when I know my friends and I like to read about a whole host of topics. Unfortunately, we usually have to go to different forms of media to get bits and pieces. I think *SELENE* could change that."

"I think you're right. And it's why we're looking to do a restart. We've had moderate success over these past few years, but I'm hoping to revamp our social media outputs, our website and even some of the sections in the magazine. This position would be working with me and would most likely be twofold—serving as a vertical editor for the website, but also contributing a small section to the magazine around current events and their effects on women."

"Honestly, that's one of the main draws for me. I have so many ideas for ways to integrate content, and I'm passionate about the fact that politics encompasses a mixture of impacts on people. One month we could talk about the fight for women's reproductive rights and look into the ideas on both sides of the table. The next month could be about domestic violence and the fact that while it's so prevalent, it's still not really discussed among women. And the very next month we could discuss the viability of women's sports or intersectional feminism and the different ways women experience the consequences of say, environmental sexism or dating."

"Wow, from environmental sexism to dating, all around sociopolitics. That's quite the range. But I like it. When people think of dating in a women's magazine, it's usually stuff that's fun and light and playful. And we'll obviously still have that section for our magazine and that vertical on the site. But I really enjoy the spin that even our dating lives are affected by the political environment of today. I see that you've really thought about what you could do in this position," she said, flashing that same smile I saw when I first met her.

"To be honest, this position is a dream come true, Alexandra. I know it's not perfect, and it will be hard work. But that's part of what I love about it, too—having the opportunity to help build on the foundation that's already there and create magic together."

"Reagan, I like what I'm hearing from you," she said. "I think the only thing left is for me to say that we'd love to have you here with us."

"Wow, really?" I asked in shock. I'd literally never been offered a position within an interview, so even though I could tell we'd clicked, I imagined she'd need to wait another couple weeks before getting back to me.

"Absolutely."

"I...am thankful. Is it okay if I get back to you by the end of the week?"

"Yes, of course. And you can always contact me if you have any questions before you decide," she said, standing up and walking us back to the conference room door. I was fairly certain I was going to accept the position, but since I'd never been offered a job on the spot before, I needed to get home, think through my options and the opportunity and make sure this was the one.

Back in the lobby, we shook hands again as Alexandra reiterated her excitement and her hope that she'd hear from me soon to let her know I'd accepted the position. We'd had a great chemistry and connection from the first time I spoke to her on the phone, and today's interview had only solidified that for her.

"What size shoe do you wear, though?" she asked, a twinkle in her eye revealing her intrigue.

"An eight," I giggled. It was totally a question I would have asked as well.

"Be glad it's not a nine or I might have to take those from you the next time we see each other."

"Depending on the shoe, I have to wear a nine sometimes, so I'll be sure to watch my back from now on anyway." *From now on.* Just then, I caught myself. As Alexandra chuckled to herself, I realized I didn't need to go home and fill out a list of pros and cons about whether I wanted this job. I knew it already. I just needed to get out of my head and go for it. Before she could turn back around and head into those glass elevators, I stopped her.

"Actually, Alexandra…what if I accepted the position now?"

"Really?" she asked.

"Yeah, I just realized I don't need to overthink this. I said it was a dream come true, so why wait?"

"That's great, Reagan. Oh, I'm very excited. I'll need to inform my HR department, but if you can come by in the next couple days, we can formalize this pretty quickly, have you sign your paperwork and figure out a start date. How does that sound for you?"

"Wonderful," I said, the smile on my face growing with every second. This had been the moment I was waiting for, where the sacrifice paid off. And like Christine said, when it happened, it felt glorious. "I can come back Friday, if that works for you."

"That's perfect. Welcome aboard, Reagan. I hope you're ready for the ride."

I watched as Alexandra walked back onto the elevator, following her stride again. It was as if she'd been a model in a former life and every floor was her runway. And she was going to be *my* new boss. I couldn't wait. Finally, I turned around and made my way out of the building, desperately trying to keep my composure, but wanting to jump into the air or dance around in circles, call my friends and squeal—something!

Holding it together as best I could, I hopped back into the Metro station and waited until I was on the train before I let out a silent squeal and stomped my shoes like a praise dancer in my seat. Things were finally starting to come together. It was just the job, yes, but it was the first thing that had gone right since working on my risk list, and I knew it had to be the start of more. I also knew there was one person I needed to see—Christine. She had to hear the good news in person.

On my way to the hospital, I shot off a few texts to the other girls and to my mom, letting them know I'd said yes to my dream job. Then an email to Alexandra, thanking her once again for meeting me and that I'd see her on Friday. All that was left was to break the news to Chrissy. My heart couldn't stop pounding with anticipation.

Back at the hospital, I fast walked in my heels to get to Christine's floor as fast as I could. She'd been right all along, and I needed her to hear from me that as much as she had inspired me to keep fighting for my happiness, she had to keep fighting for herself as well. No more talks like she was giving in. We were warriors. We fight.

I stepped off the elevator and saw Dominic walking out of her room, his head hung low. *Oh, no,* I thought. She must be having another bad day. I picked up my pace that much more and raced down the hallway, catching my breath as I neared him.

As soon as he saw me, he broke down crying and fell into my arms.

"She's gone, Rae," he cried, holding on to me tightly. "She's just…gone."

Speechless, I wrapped my arms around him and let the tears fall down my face. No way this was happening. Not right now. Not when I was on my way to remind her of all she still had left to live for.

"Where's Mama Vasquez?" I asked once my mouth could move again.

"In the room with her. They said we could stay in there while we waited for the people from the funeral home to come get her so that she could be transported to New Orleans, but I couldn't look at her any longer like that. I can't believe—"

"I know, I know. Me, either." I stood there in shock as all the years that Christine and I spent together flashed before me. It wasn't like we didn't think this day was coming, but she'd beaten her sickness so many times, I'd almost thought she was invincible. And yet, here we were, facing down the reality of life without her. *How in the world was I going to do that?*

I felt my phone vibrating in my purse and thanked it for the distraction. Looking down at it, I saw Jennifer's name as a notification on my screen along with a missed call from my mom.

Yesss girlfriend! I knew it was coming! Drinks on me this week, Jennifer had texted.

Damn. The job. I didn't have the heart to tell her or the others what had just happened, but I knew I'd have to find the strength somewhere. For now I had to go in that room and see my friend and take care of her mom. I'd figure everything else out later.

After six hours of comforting Dominic and Mama Vasquez, making sure Christine's body was transported correctly and calling our closest friends to deliver the news, I was finally home alone with no one else to take care of but me. I walked to my shoe closet, hoping that writing in my diary would help me sort out my thoughts, but once in, I dropped to the floor and cried, the pain hitting me intensely all at once.

The person who spent so much time reminding me to live was gone. *In what world was that fair?* Tears poured down as I scanned all the shoes I owned. There were easily 200 pairs of shoes in my closet, but how many of them could tell stories of me living out loud? Maybe one or two, I guessed. Certainly, my cobalt heels from last week, but that was only after Christine had helped me realize how big of a moment that had been for me. Truthfully, most were like the life I'd been living—beautiful on the outside, perfectly pristine, full of fun, sometimes embarrassing, sometimes sexy stories they could share to keep a party interesting but unfulfilled. This was what Christine had been teaching me, even trapped in the hospital for the past month: life was too short to not take it by the throat, get your shoes dirty and live with no regrets.

Before standing, my eyes caught a pair I realized I'd never worn outside my apartment. My hot pink suede, four-inch pumps from Victoria's Secret. With angel wings as pendants on the heels, they stood out as not my most expensive pair, but the lone ones without any sort of story. In fact, they'd been sitting there since I purchased them four years earlier, when I deemed them the perfect date shoes at the time. But years had passed by with no perfect date prospects and so no reason to wear them. Plus, who wanted to risk ruining the suede material on something that could turn out to be a complete bust? *What if it rained or I stepped in a puddle and it was all for naught?* I'd often thought.

"For Christine, I'm going to wear you guys very soon," I said aloud. "And it won't be on a perfect date. I'm just going to wear you." It was a promise I knew I'd have to keep.

It was time for a change; a real one this time with less complaining, less pouting about things not always going my way and less worrying about perfection. Christine had all but told me this as her last wish, and I was damn sure going to honor it. For her. And for me.

I stood up with tears still in my eyes and walked into my bedroom, opened my laptop and began retyping the risks from my list. I wouldn't be able to rip it out of my journal this time and toss it away if something went wrong. No, this time I was making a commitment to get them done and make sure the shoes I bought as my rewards lived as incautiously as Christine had been begging me to do for at least the past couple years.

Chapter Fifteen

Walking into Christine's home church in New Orleans was quite possibly one of the hardest things I've ever had to do. And it was probably why, even though we were running late for the funeral, I hesitated before entering. I stood still, trying to face what was to come, staring at those wooden doors for what seemed like hours but was only probably a few seconds. In that span of time it felt like I would never be able to move from that spot again. And I certainly didn't think I'd be able to face the fact that the woman who'd been my best friend for over a decade would be lying in a casket when I made my way in.

Standing there, in quiet frustration, I wanted so desperately to move and be strong for everyone else like normal, but I was frozen in my tracks. Finally, after some careful nudging by Jennifer and my mom, both flanking me to the left and right, I began inching my way closer to those big wooden doors of that itty-bitty church. An itty-bitty church hosting the funeral of a larger-than-life woman. To say it took that nudge, me talking myself through it and God for me to move, is probably still an understatement.

"Just put one foot in front of the other," I quietly reminded myself. "You can do this. One foot in front of the other. Repeatedly."

I looked down at the shoes that were carrying me on my journey: a pair of black sandals with a three-and-a-half-inch heel and leopard-print fabric that laced around your ankles to create a bow. As soon as I saw them in the store, I knew they were the shoes for Christine's funeral. She loved leopard print, for one, and two—she would have appreciated that the first thing I wore them to wasn't a cute and funny outing, but something dark and hurtful. Christine didn't believe in living a life that avoided pain, and I was trying to learn from her.

Besides, we had the whole tribe with us today to help us get through all of our feelings. Along with my mom and Jennifer were also Jenn's boyfriend, Robin, Rebecca and her husband, all three of my siblings and even miraculously, my dad. Together we walked to the front of the church, tiptoeing into the congregation hall that was already packed with people dressed in what I presumed were their Sunday bests: pressed blue, black and gray suits from the men, knee-length A-line skirts and dresses from some of the women, pencil skirts with suit blazers from the others. When we reached the bronze casket Mama Vasquez had insisted on for her baby, I nearly lost it. There she was, twenty-nine, full of so much life just a week ago, and now lying in a casket. Never getting the chance to marry her guy, to grow old with some kids, to become Tia Chrissy to mine. *How was any of this okay?*

The only thing that stopped me from falling apart was Mama Vasquez. Sitting in her pew to the right, she was the picture of strength as person after person flooded her and Dominic with condolences. If she could make it through today, then so could I. I straightened up my back, took in a deep breath, ran my hands down my black pencil skirt, finding courage from somewhere unknown to approach her as well.

"Querida," she cried out as I grabbed her and held on.

"I'm so, so sorry, Mama Vasquez."

"No lo sientas, mija. I hurt so much, *pero sé que ella está en paz.* You must remember that, *bueno."* She grabbed my face with both hands and stared into my eyes until I nodded. Clearly, mom and daughter were one and the same.

I hugged her tightly once more and walked to a pew a few rows behind them, watching as she had similar exchanges with Jennifer, Robin and Rebecca. *What kind of strength does it take for a mother to bury her only child and be there for others as they grieve?* I was in awe but wished she could simply be there and mourn her baby instead. As we sat, I felt my mom take my hand in hers, and it was a feeling I didn't realize I needed. Maria's comfort couldn't have come at a better time because instantly, the tears began to fall down my cheeks. With her sincere touch, I could no longer hold them in, and it seemed like the waterworks would never stop.

"I love you," I whispered, facing her, my eyes soaked.

"You could feed the whole world with the amount of love I have for you, my firstborn." She squeezed my hand and smiled. "You got that?"

"Yeah, I got that."

By the time our whole crew sat down in the pew I'd chosen and the one behind me, the opening prayer and first reading were just about to begin.

"We gather here today to say farewell to our dear Christine Vasquez, and to commit her into the hands of God," the priest said, looking into the crowd and then compassionately at Mama Vasquez. "I've known Christine since she was a little girl, so this won't be easy for me, either. But God is with us, and we are with each other." He cleared his throat before continuing, "The grace and peace of God our Father, who raised Jesus from the dead, be always with you."

"And also with you," the crowd responded.

"We'll now have our first reading from the Book of Ecclesiastes by Dominic Ríchard."

As Dominic walked slowly up to the podium, I felt my dad's strong, firm hand grip my shoulder from the pew behind me. Between him and my mom, whose hand I was still holding, maybe I could get through this funeral mass after all.

Later that evening I lay in my mom's bed, my heels kicked off and placed on the floor near her nightstand. We'd had a full day, and although I could hear my brother, sisters and my dad joking around and reminiscing about Christine as they ate crawfish at our dining room table, I needed time to simply lie down for a bit and take it all in. Sitting next to me, my mom calmly placed her hand on my head, enticing me to crawl closer and lay my head in her lap. She ran her fingers through my hair and softly sang a few verses of her favorite calming songs while my breathing steadied and my tears soaked her pants leg.

"Everything's going to be okay, Rae," she said. "But you feel as much of it as you need to right now, *cher*. I'm here, and I can take it."

I closed my eyes and listened to her as she continued on. "I just miss her so much already, Mom. What am I going to do without her?"

"You'll do what she asked you to do. You'll live and you'll honor her every time you are scared and still do something. And it'll hurt for a long time. And time won't heal that pain. I don't care what people say. But what will happen is you'll have some good days and some bad, and at some point the good days will outweigh. I won't lie to you. You will have moments when that pain is just as hard as it is today. And when that happens, you do what you're doing right now all over again—feel it, Rae. Let yourself grieve. And then it'll get good again."

"And what if it never gets good?"

"Oh, baby, it will. I can't tell you when, but it will. I just don't want this to stop the really good progress you've been making this past year. You don't think I noticed, but I have seen a different woman in front of me."

"I've been scared ninety percent of the time, Mom."

"That's okay, because it means you've already been doing it scared. I know you think you have to be perfect for everyone, Rae. But this year where I've seen you make mistakes and get hurt and get back up, it's the proudest I've ever been of my firstborn. It couldn't have been easy quitting your job and handling whatever it was that happened with you and Luke, much less watching as your best friend slowly deteriorated before your eyes. I know you've been hurt more than we could ever see down here—but you got up every time. Every single time. And you'll do it again and keep doing it."

"Because it's worth it…that's what Christine said two weeks ago while we sat and laughed in her hospital room. That it was all worth it." I turned my head to face my mom, still lying in her lap, but suddenly needing to see her eyes as we talked.

"She was right," she said, still running her fingers through my hair. "And I'm going to try to be more understanding and less demanding when you call me for help. I know you don't always like when I offer my advice, even if it is usually very good." She couldn't help herself adding in the last part with a chuckle.

"Never change, Mom. I need you just like you are. Just like this."

I turned my head back to face the TV as my mom continued singing, and my eyes caught my shoes again, standing up tall near her nightstand. It was then that I realized one more important thing: these were my third pair of shoes from the list. I could finally officially mark off "allow people to be there for me." Christine would be oh so proud.

Chapter Sixteen

"What do you girls want to drink?" Robin asked from her kitchen. "Because we definitely need drinks!"

"You have some bourbon?" I asked. "I could definitely go for a whiskey ginger about now."

"Do you even have to ask me that?" She poked her head out the door to the living room where Jennifer and I were sitting around the gray tufted ottoman she used as her coffee table. "Of course I have bourbon. And I have ginger ale. Is that good with you, Jenn?"

"Absolutely. But don't judge me, because I'm probably going to need several tonight."

"No judgment," I said. "Trust."

Robin walked into her living room in the most Robin-est way, carrying a round silver serving tray with handles. On top of it stood three whiskey glasses, a bottle of Maker's Mark bourbon and a two-liter of ginger ale.

"Never," she said, putting the tray on top of the ottoman. Carefully lifting each glass off the tray, she gave us our first pours. We heard the crackle from the bourbon hitting the coldness of the frozen whiskey stones she'd placed in the glasses while in the kitchen. And then the calming fizzle from the soda joining in. It was amazing how the simplest sounds made so much noise two days after burying your best friend.

"To Christine," I said, lifting my glass up for a toast.

"To Christine," Robin and Jennifer said, joining in.

"May you continue to rest in peace. We sure do miss you, *mana*."

"And we'll drink one extra of these since you can't," Robin added.

We clanked our glasses together and took huge gulps of our drinks, almost finishing what we had in one swallow. I closed my eyes and sat back as some of the memories between us flashed through me, breathing in deeply and remembering what my mom had said about allowing myself to feel everything that came with grief when it did. Robin lay fully down on her couch, stretching her body the length of it, and watched me and Jennifer as Jenn curled her arms around her legs and soothingly rocked herself back and forth. The three of us sat just like that, in silence for about five minutes, until Robin broke the ice.

"Anyone need another pour?"

"Yes, please," I said, jumping out of my position. "You know, I remember that Memorial Day party we went to some years back and how much whiskey we had that night. Oh, it was crazy, and Christine was, of course, the life of the party—what was the name of it again?"

"The Pumps and a Bump party?" Robin asked as she made us more drinks.

"Yes! That was the one. What an awful name."

"It was kind of an awful party, too," Jennifer said.

"No, it wasn't." I took a sip of my drink while disagreeing. "We had a blast. I can still hear Christine's booming voice piercing through the noise at that party. '*Manas!* Come, sit, drink.' She was in her element that night. That was, what, a couple years after college?"

"Yeah, I think so," said Robin. "I remember the horrible outfits everyone had on that night. You had on, like, a multicolored, plunging one-piece bathing suit, and I wore a silver metallic two-piece that barely covered my butt. Oh, God, those were so awful!"

"They really were! And Chrissy had on some booty shorts with a fire-red bikini top. What were we thinking?" I laughed, taking another sip and sitting back again.

"We weren't. That's the point," Jennifer said.

"That party was like the Black version of *Eyes Wide Shut*. You only liked it because you got laid that night."

"One, I didn't get laid *thank you very much*. And you only hated it because you didn't! There were so many fine men that night. You could have had your pick, but that's not what you were on."

"It certainly wasn't."

"Okay," I said, rolling my eyes. "My point was just that's one of the times I recall Chrissy having fun before she ever got sick and had that damn procedure in the first place."

"That was a fun night, Rae. I agree," Robin said. "Especially the part where we had to help your drunk ass try to find the shoe you lost after rolling around in the hay with some rando."

"All right, no need to bring that part up."

"Christine couldn't stop laughing at you. She was like, 'Oh, I know Reagan is dying about her precious shoe.' Can't believe we never found it, too."

"Ugh, I know. RIP to that heel," I said, imitating as if I would pour some of my drink on the floor "for my homie." "I learned a valuable lesson that night."

"What was that?" Jennifer asked.

"No man, not even one who just wants to eat you out for hours with no reciprocation, is worth the cost of a lost shoe."

"Girl, bye! I can't cosign that," Robin screamed out.

"No, I'm serious!"

"I know you are, but I am, too. Screw those shoes. I'll take the hours-long eating fest."

Robin and Jennifer high-fived each other and cracked up laughing.

"Oh, you agree with that, but was just ragging on me about the actual party?" I asked, looking at Jennifer.

"Hey, what can I say? I'm a complicated woman."

"Indeed," I said, shaking my head.

"The memory I keep coming back to was meeting you and Christine for the first time in college. I thought you two were inseparable, and I'd never be able to live up to that friendship for either of you."

"Oh, Jennifer, I didn't know you felt that way."

"I mean, you two had those wallet-size photos you took together in high school and would use them to give out your phone numbers to guys. Photos with both of you in the picture! How was anyone supposed to compete with that?"

"Well, that was a foolish idea of ours anyway, and it only worked like maybe once or twice. Most of the time the guys didn't remember which one he'd met the night before and wasn't sure which girl he was calling when he did…all that to say, it was just us not knowing what we were doing in college. Not some impenetrable bond."

"No, I know that…now. But initially, when we met in the dorms, I didn't think there was any space for anyone else. It wasn't until Christine pulled me aside one day and told me I was one of the few people she felt comfortable being herself around outside home that I knew we were all really starting to become friends. That was maybe end of sophomore year?"

"You spent almost two years thinking we weren't actually friends?"

"More like just not believing the extent of the friendship. Like I said, complicated."

"Oh, friend." I leaned over and grabbed Jennifer's hand. She had always been the sensitive one of our group, but I hadn't realized how far that sensitivity went until then. To think she ever thought she meant less than everything to me and Christine was just too much to take.

"I know, I know. I'm crazy. This is why I say everyone needs therapy."

"It's worked for me so far," Robin chimed in. "Matter of fact, I need to make sure I still have my appointment this week. I am definitely going to need to talk some stuff out, okay?"

"I know that's right," I replied. "We're going to all need to keep talking, too, honestly. Especially as May nears and what would have been Christine's thirtieth birthday comes around."

"Ugh, that reminds me. We were talking about her joining me for another of my work trips to London one of the last times I visited her in the hospital," Robin said. "She knew I had a trip coming up, and you know she was on her live-out-loud kick, so

I told her she should come. She was so excited to get out of that hospital and join me."

"You think she really thought she was going to be able to go?" I asked, vividly recalling our conversation where she'd admitted to me that she felt like she was dying. I hadn't told anyone about that belief at the time because it felt too personal, but I wasn't sure if she'd relayed the same sentiment to any of the other girls.

"She was trying to. I know she didn't think she had a lot of time left, and she wanted to make sure if she saw thirty, she saw it in style."

"That sounds about right," Jennifer said.

"You know, now that I think about it, you guys are more than welcome to come, too, you know."

"Come to London?" Jennifer asked.

"Yeah. Why not? I'll have to work, obviously, but if we time it just right, you all could come to London for my last few days and then we could hop over to Paris for another few. Just live it up in honor of Chrissy."

"I like that idea a lot," I said.

"And you're there at least three times a year, so you could be our tour guide," Jennifer added as she started calculating the possibility in her head.

"Exactly. I have to leave next week, but we could look up what flights look like in May, and if they are reasonable, you guys should really come. I would love it."

"Let's do it," I said, jumping up again.

"Really?"

"Yeah, like you said, why not?"

"Okay!"

"All right, I'm down, too," Jennifer said. "No way I'm letting you two go on this trip without me."

"Yes!" Robin leaped up from her couch and began dancing. "I think this is going to be so good. We're going to have tons of fun. I'm a little surprised you didn't need to make a pros and cons list about it before deciding, but I'm going to take it. No backing out now," she said, pointing to me.

"No more pros and cons lists!" I said, laughing. "I've got a spontaneous checkmark to fill out."

"Ooooh, someone's back on the risk list?" Jennifer asked.

"Indeed I am."

"Good, I'm glad to hear that."

"I'll have to figure out how it works with the new job, but that should be easy enough. I'll just tell Alexandra I had a trip already planned before accepting the job. She feels like the kind of person who would understand."

"Ohhhh, yes, the new job!" Robin yelled out again. "In all the death and funeral madness, we never properly celebrated your big win. I'm so sorry."

"Please, it's not like we could have done that before now. And seems to me London and Paris are a great place to celebrate."

"Ha! Very true," Jennifer said.

"Okay, then it's settled. You two look up flights

and let me know as soon as you can when you want to come. I'll be free after the first week of May."

"Perfect."

"And in the meantime, we need another drink. This time to Chrissy and to Reagan. I see big things coming for you, *chica*," Robin said, pouring whiskey into each of our glasses once more.

"To Chrissy and Rae," Jennifer said, raising her glass. "And big things coming."

"For us all," I added with a wink.

Chapter Seventeen

Stepping out of the airport in London, I immediately felt the cool, crisp air and was all too happy to be wearing my new navy blue Joules knee-high flat boots. While the temperature had begun warming up back in DC, London was still firmly in the fifties, especially at the break of dawn. It didn't hurt that I was also simply in love with these shoes: with the cute little red bow in the back of them tied around a gold buckle on the outside portion of your calf, jazzing up what could have been just a plain blue boot.

By the time I saw Robin and Jennifer outside waiting for me, I was in full happy travels mode. Initially wanting to do something silly like throw my hat in the sky à la Mary Tyler Moore, I ultimately decided to take in a deep breath and release the biggest twirl I could imagine while shouting out "I am here!" It didn't even matter that people were watching. This was *my* way of releasing all the pressures I'd been mounting on myself for the past several months, maybe even years.

"Reagan, you are so crazy," I heard Robin scream out to my left just as I was rounding my third twirl.

"Aggggh. Hey, girls!" I ran toward them and hugged them both tightly.

"What in the world were you doing?" Jennifer asked.

"Dancing! You want to join?"

"Uh, no, thanks," they said in unison, unable to hold in their laughter.

"How about we just get you and your stuff to the car, and we can dance later tonight," Jennifer added through her fit of chuckles.

"Wait, we have a car? Ooh, y'all are fancy."

"Nah, don't say *y'all*. Robin is fancy, but then she always has been. No surprise there."

"That's true."

"Uh, no, Robin has been in London for the past two weeks and she needed a car for things like grocery shopping," Robin chimed in, speaking in third person as if it would help her case.

"Grocery shopping and picking folks up from the airport, you mean," Jennifer clarified.

"Right. I feel like I've used the car more for that than anything else, honestly."

"Who else have you had to pick up?"

"Who haven't I come to get is probably an easier question to answer. I didn't realize how many people I invited to London this time around, and nearly everyone took me up on my offer. My parents stopped in for two days on their way to Amsterdam and Belgium, Rebecca and her husband came through on their way to see his people in Scotland, Lance and Candice came for a day before heading to Paris and even my hairdresser stayed for an extended layover."

"And you picked them all up?"

"I'm a glutton for punishment," she said, jokingly hanging her head in shame.

"Good thing, then, that you can turn this car in forever in about three days, since we'll be off to Paris!" I made sure to say Paris where it sounds like Par-eeh, because I'm *cultured*, and was maybe a little tipsy from the whiskey gingers I had on the plane.

"Yes," Robin screamed out excitedly. "Now, that's something I can dance about."

"Oh, yeah." My ears perked up.

"No, no, no, that still doesn't mean here. Let's get your bags and go," Jennifer said, interrupting my would-be triumph to get them, or at least Robin, to join me.

"Fine, we can do that, too," I responded defiantly.

"If it makes you feel any better, I think your boots are super cute."

"Thanks, girl, they are another reward from the list." I twirled around once more for effect.

"Okay, see? Come on, now. I just told you later,"

Jennifer said, bursting out laughing. "Got these people looking at us like we're crazy."

"Whatever. Let them look. I'm tired of caring what other people think about what makes me happy," I countered, grabbing my bag and turning my twirl into a skip.

As we approached the car, I noticed the sun was finally starting to come out. While the weather had been slightly overcast when I deplaned, it had dramatically changed in the hours since then, and the sun was shining brightly through the clouds.

"Where to first, girls?" I asked as we packed the car with my luggage.

"We need to bring your things back to my flat, and then we can go wherever you want."

"Oh, that's a no-brainer, then. We have to start at Buckingham Palace," Jennifer responded.

"Agreed. Definitely the palace," I added with a high five to Jennifer.

"All right, then, first stop on the Robin Johnson London Tour—my flat. Second stop—Buckingham Palace! Prince Harry, we're coming for you, boo." Robin started up her car and pointed her hand in the direction of what we guessed was her flat or at least something close to it. But Jennifer was stuck on the Prince Harry part, and couldn't let it go.

"First of all, isn't he married?" she asked.

"Don't hate! I can still look and dream about having a royal wedding, damn it."

"And, also not here! He and Meghan moved to the US, remember?"

"Oh, damn, that's right."

We all fell out laughing. If this was what the whole trip would be like, I was going to need stitches for my stomach when we returned to the States just from giggling so much. I only wished Christine could have been there with us.

The next ten hours went by like a blur. We walked what seemed like every street in London, stopping to take silly photos at everything from Buckingham Palace to Big Ben, Westminster Abbey and more. We saw the grandeur of the old buildings in Europe and marveled at the seamless mixture of old Victorian architecture with pointed arches and steep roofs and modern skyscrapers slowly but surely changing the landscape of the city. And with each place we went to, I made sure to feature my boots prominently in every picture for the Gram.

The day before, I'd decided that I would take my shoe-of-the-day posts to the next level for this trip and chronicle every part of it, not just once a day, showing the ups and downs and funny and ugly parts about traveling. Not leaving out the ugly bits, like Christine would say. Sometimes I jumped up high and kicked my boots in the air. Other times I posed as if I was kicking down a building. But I started the day by taking an introspective photo of my shoes walking down the pathway to Buckingham Palace that was dedicated to Princess Diana and showing how I'd accidentally stepped in some gum. *Talk about apropos.*

"Wow, dahling," Robin mocked in her very bad, very fake, British accent. "The uni-verse certainly wanted to welcome our dear Reagan to this city of luxury in the oddest of ways." She spread out her arms to emphasize her point about the grandeur surrounding us.

"Is this the same universe that is supposedly matching you up with a very married, very not here, Prince Harry?" I asked. "Because if so—"

"Don't be such a jerk," Robin interrupted, pretending to be upset.

"What?" I asked. "I'm just saying that it might possibly be a long shot."

"Whatever. You never know," Robin responded, but I could see that her attention had been distracted by a horse-drawn carriage riding past us on the street. *Now, this was some real deal London extravagance.* The three of us watched, enthralled as the carriage came to an alarming stop right outside the palace gates, almost like what happens when someone realizes in the middle of walking out of their apartment that they forgot something. This was what it looked like we were watching take place in front of our very eyes. But what prince or princess forgot something just as they were entering the gates?

We slowly tried to inch ourselves closer in an attempt to see if someone was getting out; none of us saying a word but moving in sync with each other. We noticed the man on the horse get down, reach into the carriage and slowly but assuredly begin walking toward us. Frozen, we watched as that same man walked straight up to Robin.

"Good afternoon, miss," he said, slightly bowing his head.

"Good afternoon," Robin replied and then curtsied.

The man smiled politely, but you could tell he wanted to laugh at the American curtseying in such a nonformal situation.

"Prince Eric has asked me to give you this note."

"Oh?"

"Yes, madam."

Robin reached for the note, opened it and let out a very big grin. "Please tell Mr. Eric thank you, and that I will be sure to do so."

"Thank you, ma'am."

The gentleman turned back around as quickly as he walked up to us and headed back to his horse. In awe, we watched as he mounted the horse again and drove the carriage through the palace gates. It wasn't until it was completely out of sight that Jennifer and I turned our attention to Robin.

"Ummmm, what the hell just happened?" Jennifer asked, being the first one to break the silence.

"I think Robin's ass just got asked out by a damn prince," I shouted with glee.

"It would appear so. Is that what just happened, Robin?"

"No comment," Robin replied, smiling harder than I'd seen from her since I arrived in London. She folded the paper up and put it into her purse without saying another word.

"Seriously? No comment?" I asked.

"Nope. So maybe we should change the subject. Are you guys ready to go to the London Eye?"

"Yeah, sure, whatever," Jennifer said drily. "Let's do the London Eye and not talk about the craziness that just went down in front of us. Because that makes sense."

"But don't think this is the end of this conversation," I interjected.

"And don't think you can say I told you so, either," Jennifer corrected. "It's still not Prince Harry."

We all busted out laughing again and walked to our next destination.

After about thirty minutes of walking and trying to get more information out of Robin, we finally reached the London Eye. Seeing the huge observation wheel in front of us, it seemed to jut into the clouds, making it a magical sight to see even from below. It was also somehow in the perfect placement for viewing, being just to the side on the River Thames, across from Big Ben.

"Well, ladies, let's do this," I said, walking up to the line to board the wheel.

As we waited, the conversation turned to me since

Robin had only given up that "it was a nice note" from all our prying on the walk over.

"Rae, are you liking the new job?" Robin asked.

"You know what? I really am," I said. "I'm not going to lie, I have been super nervous about making a good impression and not falling flat on my face, but I'm also pretty excited to see if I have what it takes."

"I get that. Totally. First time my job sent me here as the ambassador for our European sales team, I damn near threw up in my flat every morning before I went to work. But at the same time, I couldn't have been more excited to be doing what I always said I wanted to do."

"That's exactly it! And the fact that I've wanted it for so long makes it that much scarier. It's like, okay I can't mess up the thing I've been asking for forever."

"Ha ha, right," Robin agreed. "But you got this. You know this stuff in and out. I have no doubt you're going to soar."

"And at the very least, we don't have to worry about job searching on Friday nights anymore," Jennifer added. "At least not for a while."

"Hell, yeah. I hate job searching. But more than that, I just hated how I'd let so many things get in my head this year. Making that change from playing it safe to jumping out there on everything threw me for a bit of a loop at first. I think I'm starting to get the hang of it now, though."

We walked farther through the line, inching our way closer to the actual wheel.

"Does this mean you've let go of those nasty things Matthew said to you earlier this year, too... and the disappointment of Luke?" Robin asked.

"You know what? I hope so. I realized after that he was just Matthew being Matthew. And with Luke, I think I'd put so much pressure on that situation to work because I wanted him to be the perfect foil to Jake. And the moment he didn't live up to that, it crushed me. Truth is, he was simply another guy who didn't live up to expectations, not the referendum on dating and love that it felt like in the moment. I don't know why I'd expected more from either of them, to be honest."

"Because we all make the mistake of expecting more," Robin replied. "And then find ourselves extremely disappointed when they don't live up to it."

"So true," Jennifer added.

"Mmm-hmm," Robin agreed again.

"What do *you* mean, *mmm-hmm*?" I asked, turning to Robin.

"*Whaaaaaat?* I get a secret letter from a prince and all of a sudden I can't agree about men being trash sometimes?" She put her hand to her chest as if she was really offended.

"Yes. That's pretty much exactly what it means," I replied. "You have nothing to say in this conversation from here through the rest of the trip."

"Hmph, Jennifer's got a whole boyfriend and she gets to cosign."

"But mine isn't a secret prince."

Robin fake stomped her feet onto one of the passenger capsules and finally gave in to the peer pressure. "Whatever. You know I'll tell you guys the deal later." She turned around to face us after she entered. "Just know that Eric is someone who has reminded me that none of my success means anything without someone to share it with."

"Aww," Jennifer said with a sigh. "We surely can't wait to finally get these details then, girl."

"And y'all will…just later. In the privacy of my home. Promise."

"All right," we responded in unison.

Jennifer and I walked into the capsule behind her, one by one, and prepared our minds as it began to lift into the sky. It was one of the most gorgeous and breathtaking sights we'd ever seen. Up, up and up we went, first glancing at places like St. Paul's Cathedral and the business district, then the Tower of London and the Palace of Westminster as we continued traveling in a circle overlooking the city. We also saw the top of Big Ben and could just make out what looked to be Trafalgar Square, but it was the beauty of the river and the chain of parks stretching from the Palace Gardens to Kensington Palace that caught all our breaths.

I couldn't stop thinking about Robin and her prince, though. It was funny how the woman I considered to be the most career focused of us all was the one who seemed to secretly have been following her heart while in London, maybe every time she came here. I glanced over at her and suddenly saw my friend in a totally different light. Sure, she was still take-no-mess-from-anyone Robin, but what if she had also been becoming live-your-life-with-no-regrets Robin and I'd just not noticed because I'd been in my head the whole time? More important, she made it very clear she wasn't looking for our approval or our feedback. It was refreshing, and just like Christine used to do, challenged me a bit. *What prince had I been missing out on all this time?*

"Wow," I said, leaning on Jennifer's shoulder and refocusing on the sights in front of us. "This might be one of the most beautiful things I've ever seen."

"Completely agreed."

"And I couldn't be happier that I'm seeing it with you girls."

"Completely agreed," Robin mimicked. "Now, let's get a picture of the three of us on here before it's time to get off."

"Oh, yes," I said, pulling out my phone so it could go on the Gram as well. I approached the nearest couple and asked them to take our photo.

"Say cheese," exclaimed the woman behind her beau as he positioned my phone to get the best angle of us.

"Cheese!"

Three days later I had on my favorite low-top Chuck Taylors as we traipsed down the Champs-élysées. Surprisingly, it was even more beautiful than our view on the London Eye with its mixture of high-fashion stores and history. If you looked straight down the avenue, you could see the Arc de Triomphe standing massively in its own existence, waiting for you to visit it. But in between that and the Place de la Concorde stood cinemas and cafés by the dozens, luxury shops and the grandest greenery you could see bordering the sidewalk.

We'd just left the Louis Vuitton store when we noticed a young couple that looked as if they'd just been married. He was dressed in a black tuxedo; she in a mermaid-cut ivory gown with crystals on the bodice. Their photographer, bless his heart, was attempting to guide them into different poses, but the two of them just keep staring at each other and smiling.

"Okay, now release each other's hands, and you caress her face," the photographer yelled out to no avail as the two lovebirds remained in their own world no matter how hard he tried to get their attention.

"Excusez-moi," he said in a very thick French accent, all the while still getting ignored. It was as if the couple had completely forgotten they were supposed to be taking pictures.

"Ahem, *pardon.*" He cleared his throat and tried speaking louder. "We're going to miss this sunset if you two don't work with me here."

"Oh, no, we're so sorry, sir," the woman cried out with a slight Texas accent. "I simply can't get over the fact that I married the love of my life. In Paris!"

She squealed, and her husband grabbed her up in a familiar embrace, prompting the photographer to finally relent and begin taking candid photos of them.

"We'll do better, I promise," she said, giving him her best attempt at puppy eyes.

"That's okay. That's okay. These will do just fine. *Mais oui?*"

Watching from afar, I guessed the sad eyes must have worked or the photographer was simply tired of being ignored and decided to give in to what was in front of him. Either way, it looked like all parties were finally getting what they wanted out of the photo shoot. The photographer, his shots in the sunset. The couple, more chances to play around with each other on the streets of Paris. It reminded me of how I'd seen Candice and Lance holding on to each other at their wedding. And the undeniable chemistry of a couple who's in love.

Just like then, I felt a certain sadness grow inside me that hit like a ton of bricks even as I stood there happy for the couple in front of me. But unlike then, I was determined to not let love pass me by anymore. Rebecca and Christine's words flooded my consciousness as I remembered them both persuading me to take a chance on giving my heart to someone again. Things with Luke had admittedly stalled that progress, made me believe that living my life cautiously, afraid of the other shoe dropping at any moment, was better than feeling the knife to my heart when he left me at that ball. But I had been wrong.

Playing it safe all these years hadn't stopped the pain from coming or made it hurt less; it just either made me numb or far too excited about a prospect before really getting to know him, and ultimately caused me to miss out on the kind of happiness this couple was allowing themselves to experience.

"Reagan?" I heard Robin call my name in the background, jolting me out of my thoughts. "Looked like you were in your own world there for a second."

"Yeah, I guess I was. But I'm good now."

"You sure?"

"I'm sure. I was just having a moment, watching that couple and thinking about redoing my try at being vulnerable with a guy again. Not just to check it off on a list, though. But to give someone a real chance this time and also not rush it into being something perfect before we really get to know each other."

"I'm really glad to hear you say that, Rae. In fact, maybe you should know that I've been talking to Jake nonstop since your blow up at the hospital. He called me later that night when he calmed down and realized he never actually saw Christine that day, but still wanted to know how she was doing. He's been a wreck since then, trying to figure out what he can do to apologize and win your trust again. He even came to the funeral, but decided at the last minute he didn't want to make things worse by letting you know."

"What?" I was floored once again by Robin in a matter of three days.

"I know. I didn't say anything because I wasn't sure you were ready. Plus, once Christine passed, it just didn't feel like the right time. But that man loves you. He hasn't always expressed that like he should, and he needs to do better with that—which I've told him over and over again. But he does love you. And I know you still love him. That's why that fight hurt so much."

"I don't know, Robin," I said with a sigh. "No man has ever hurt me as much as he has. Am I really going to put myself in the position to be destroyed by him again?"

"If you think the risk is worth it, yeah."

Those words stuck with me as we raced to catch up to Jennifer, who'd flagged down a taxi cab so we could get to the Eiffel Tower before it lit up at night.

"Pouvez-vous nous prendre à la Tour Eiffel, s'il vous plaît," Jennifer said to the driver as we hopped in the backseat of the car.

"What did you say to him?" Robin asked.

"Can you take us to the Eiffel Tower, please."

"Ohhhhh, fancy, *oui oui.*"

"Mock all you want. But when we get there on time to see those lights, I don't want to hear a word. The sun's already setting and you two were, what, gazing lovingly at some strange couple?"

"Maybe a little more than that, but you're right, we need to stay on track," I said, nodding to Robin on the side about our little inside conversation. "I also want to get some crepes across the street while we watch."

"Oh, and some mulled wine," Robin added.

"Any other requests you all want to add as we're crunched for time?" Jennifer asked jokingly.

"Nope, that pretty much covers it. I'm just ready to see and experience it all," I said, staring blankly out the window as we passed by some of Paris's historical landmarks and saw more couples strolling the streets, hand in hand. *So this is why they call Paris the City of Love*, I thought. It had certainly made me reconsider the biggest risk of all and ask myself that age-old question: Was it worth it?

Chapter Eighteen

*D*ing. *Ding.*

I raced to the buzzer near my front door, looked in the camera and saw Jake standing outside. It was 7:15 p.m. on the dot, and he was on time for our date. *One notch in his book*, I thought.

"Hello?" I asked, speaking into the intercom system.

"Hey, it's Jake."

"I know," I said with a laugh. "Just wanted to hear you say it. Okay, hold on just a sec."

I pressed the button to open the door to my lobby entrance and then quickly attempted to compose myself one last time before he reached my door. This obviously wasn't our first date, but it was the first time we were seeing each other since our fight, and

more importantly, since I called him when I returned
from Paris. Still, even though we'd aired out our dirty
laundry and spent the majority of that call apolo-
gizing and admitting that our fears had stopped us
throughout the years, it had taken everything in me
to say yes when he asked me for this date. Only ac-
quiescing after we both agreed it would be a real
first date and not a quick speed bump to an imme-
diate relationship.

We had to learn each other again, despite years of
history behind us. I was nervous beyond belief as he
came up my steps and desperately trying not to sweat
through my blouse before he got a good look at me. I
steadied my breathing, forced myself to stop pacing
the length of my living room and took in three deep
breaths before I heard him knocking on my door.

"Jake?" I asked through the door, giving myself
some time to simultaneously remember that I was
the catch, and he was here to see me, so I could enjoy
tonight and stop wasting time on all the what-ifs
that had been swirling in my head since I'd agreed
to see him.

"That's me. The man of your dreams."

"Now that is a lofty title for someone who sped
off and left me the last time that we saw each other."

"Oh, too soon, Rae." I swung the door open with a
smile on my face and saw him posted up, pretending
as if he'd been jabbed in the gut with a knife. I knew
the feeling, but I figured I'd let his joke slide. That
had been a bit of a low blow. Besides, it would have
been hard for me to say anything in retort without

the ability to breathe. There he stood before me, the epitome of handsome, five foot eleven in a striped crewneck sweater and pants that made him look like he could be a J. Crew model, and his dimple radiating off his cheek. It was fair to say I was mesmerized by his presence and the night hadn't even begun.

"Hey there," he said, after giving me a very obvious and long once-over as well. "You look…absolutely beautiful."

The pause in between his words were for emphasis, but they were also absolutely working. I steadied my breathing again and stared into his eyes for a good twenty seconds before responding. Long enough to let him swoon, watching me stand at my door with my cream button-down blouse, black matte liquid leggings and those hot pink suede pointed-toe pumps I'd been holding in my closet for years. I forced him to gaze at me while neither of us spoke a word, knowing he enjoyed the view, and that I liked having him enjoy it.

"Thank you," I finally said and allowed him to walk in.

"So how much time do we have before we need to leave for the concert?" he asked, casually grazing my left leg with his hand as he took his shoes off at my door.

"Probably no more than about twenty minutes."

"Oh, good, that works perfectly."

"Perfectly for what?"

"For us to enjoy a little wine and some snacks,"

he replied, showing off the items that were in the bag he was holding when he came in.

"Really? Wine and strawberries?" I asked mockingly.

"What?" he asked, feigning innocence. "It's just something to drink and eat."

"Mmm-hmm, if you say so."

He winked at me and smiled. "I do. You still have a wine opener, right?"

"Oh, hi, I'm sorry, do we have to introduce ourselves because you don't know me? Of course I have a wine opener."

"I never know what could have changed in four years."

"Please. You follow me on Instagram. I know you see my posts. Don't act like because we haven't talked you don't know what's going in my life."

"You're right. I do know."

As we walked to my kitchen to open the wine, Jake wrapped his big arms around me and placed his head in the nook of my neck. It didn't make for the most elegant walk, but the smell of his cologne, with its subtle intoxication, made up for any awkwardness and almost served to put me in a trance.

"I'm so glad we're going to see Snoh Aalegra in concert together," he whispered from behind me into my right ear, the hairs on his goatee slightly grazing my neck.

"Me, too," I said breathlessly, trying to keep my composure enough to release actual words from my mouth. "I'm really looking forward to it."

"As much as these strawberries?" he asked while releasing me from his embrace as we entered the kitchen.

"Surprisingly, yes, even more than the strawberries."

"Now, that's saying something. Because *these* strawberries, I have to tell you. They are top-notch."

"It's crazy, right? Imagine me anticipating a concert more than some fruit. I mean, how could I?"

We both cracked up laughing at my sarcasm. I was mostly just happy to regain control over my wits again. There was no way I could make a decision about if it was worth it to try again if I couldn't think straight. And on top of that, I wanted tonight to be fun, not some tired version of a soap opera story where the lead character is so overcome by passion she jumps into bed with the guy and everyone watching the show wants to scream out *"Nooooooo, don't do it!"* I needed tonight to not just be about sex with him, especially after what went down at the wedding. But he surely made it hard by oozing sex with every word he spoke.

I picked up the wine opener and attempted to play keep-away from him to keep the jovial atmosphere going; standing on my tippy toes, running to the back of the kitchen and tucking the wine opener under my arm. Each time he came near me, he was very close to getting it from me, but never did.

"You know, there's only so much of this you're going to be able to do in those shoes of yours," he remarked from the other side of the kitchen with a devilish look in his eyes.

"Ha! That's where you're wrong," I said through heavy breaths from running. "I can do a lot in these heels."

"Oh, really?" he asked with a raised eyebrow.

"I didn't mean it like that, nasty."

"What? I just—" He stopped himself and started laughing again.

"You just nothing, exactly," I replied. "But since you're wondering, yes, I can do those things in these heels as well. Just not tonight."

With a sly smirk, I casually let him know that maybe there had been some things he didn't know about me in the four years since the wedding, but also that anything like that would have to be saved for his imagination.

"That's fine. Tonight is all about Snoh anyway. I wouldn't want you to sully her night."

"Sully *her* night?" I asked, incredulous at the thought, but soon realized my surprise response was exactly what he'd planned on. He'd distracted me long enough for him to take the wine opener from me and also grab me toward him.

"Just so we're clear," he said, looking at me with a sudden very intense stare. "If we continue talking about what you can do in those pink shoes, we won't make it to the concert."

"No?" I asked.

"No."

"Then we should open the wine and talk about other things, huh?"

"Yeah, I think so," he said, releasing me from his grip, but not before allowing his right hand to slide down the side of my body, and his lips to graze the side of my neck. My knees almost buckled under me, and my body betrayed me by instinctively allowing him full access.

"That won't help things, either, I'm sure," I stammered, slowly taking a few steps back from him.

"Sorry, I couldn't help myself."

His smile was so big now I could see his teeth glistening in the kitchen light, but he wasn't the only one losing control. Biting my lower lip slightly, I tried to stand back up straight, shaking that familiar chill out of my spine.

Fifteen minutes later we were still standing in my kitchen, feeding each other strawberries and drinking wine. Luckily, he'd set an alarm on his iPhone so at minute eighteen, it went off with a loud blare.

"You ready?"

"Yep. More than you know."

"Woman."

"Yes?"

"You want to go to this concert, right?"

"Yes!"

"Okay, because I'm this close to snatching you up and ravaging the hell out of you. So you better stop playing with me."

I busted out laughing, but I could tell he was serious.

"Okay, okay. Let's go. We can't leave Snoh wait-ing, and if we stay here any longer, I might end up doing something I don't want to do."

"Trust me, neither of us wants that," he said. As we gathered our things to leave, he looked down at my shoes and noticed they were suede. "You know they're saying it may rain tonight."

"Yeah, I know. But it's high time these shoes get out of the closet, rain be damned."

We stepped into DC's Constitution Hall, a popu-lar midsize concert venue, holding hands as we ma-neuvered through the crowd.

"Now, where are these seats?" I asked.

"Section B, F 7 and 8," he replied, looking down at our tickets once more.

"Oh, okay, cool."

We continued walking and looking for our sec-tion, until we'd walked almost the entire circle of the hall. Clearly, we had gone the wrong way when we entered, but I was too distracted by the handholding to have noticed or cared.

We finally got to our seats just as Snoh came onto the stage and began singing her hit song, "I Want You Around."

As the beat dropped on the song, we danced at our seats with Jake's hand sliding across the small of my back.

"I love this song," he exclaimed in between notes.

"Me, too!"

We both looked at each other knowingly, but simply continued dancing and singing.

Song after song, we joined her on her love journey. We danced in each other's arms on "Find Someone Like You." We prodded each other on "Love Like That." We let our eyes and hands roam on "Here Now." But as the concert wrapped up, I rested my head on his chest as Snoh sang what had become our theme song in my head in the days since I said yes to Jake's invite: "I Didn't Mean to Fall in Love." In my ear, Jake sang along with her, and it was like she was providing the words he'd wanted to say to me all along.

I closed my eyes and listened to them both, letting the feelings I'd been struggling to hold back for so long invade my everything. There I was, finally allowing myself to believe in the possibility of love again, believe in me and Jake of all people. And it was scary and unfamiliar, but also damn good. Unfortunately, immediately after the song ended, all my fears came rushing back into my head. *You know better than this*, I said to myself. *He's shown you that you can't trust him. Just as soon as things go too well, he's shown you—he'll bail. Why should now be any different?*

I could feel my body tense up and my chest get tight as one part of me tried to fight back the fears and the other acknowledged they were there for a reason. I slowly peeled myself from him, first my hands dropping from his chest and then lifting my head up and taking a few steps back.

"Reagan," he said with a look of concern washing over his face. "I love you. I know we have a lot to work on, and it will take time for the both of us to trust each other again. But I need you to know that it starts with me loving you—and I'm hoping the rest can fall in place. I'm ready for things to be different this time, but are you?"

I looked back at him, still unsure of what path to take and what to believe. I wanted to trust him; I wanted to be the person everyone had been pushing me to be lately, the one who was more open and willing to really take this kind of risk, but I was also so frightened of being hurt again. Especially by him. *How could I trust that he wouldn't say he loves me and then walk away again, that the long distance wouldn't get in between us, that somehow if we put in the work, these two highly imperfect people would soar instead of falling?*

A million questions ran through my head in the seconds it took for me to respond, but one voice instantly calmed them all. Christine's. "Stop living cautiously," she'd warned me. "Take some risks and be willing to fall, and when you do, just get up and try again. And it will always be worth it." This wasn't just about Jake, I realized. All of the risks had been about me learning to trust myself again, as well as my ability to get back up if things didn't work out how I'd planned. This thing with Jake was no different, but going through the rest of them helped me better know the strength I had within me and the bravery it took for me to be with him in this moment. And I didn't want that feeling to end any time soon.

Taking in one more deep breath, I paused briefly and spoke what was on my heart. "Jake. I love you, too. And things *absolutely* will be different this time, because we've both done a lot of growing, and we're not going to hold back anything from each other anymore. Which means I have to tell you I am scared to death to be with you, but it's worth it to me to acknowledge that fear and then do it anyway."

"Good," he said, taking me in his arms. "Then we can face those fears together."

* * * * *

For more great romances about grabbing for the life you really want, try these other books from Harlequin Special Edition:

Starlight and the Single Dad
By Michelle Major

A Rancher's Touch
By Allison Leigh

She Dreamed of a Cowboy
By Joanna Sims

Available now wherever Harlequin Special Edition books and ebooks are sold!

Acknowledgments

I started writing some version of *The Shoe Diaries* more than a decade ago, so to say that I have a lot of people to thank for keeping me going along the way would be an absolute understatement.

But first, I *have* to thank God. I often talk about hearing God's whispers any time I doubted if I could do this or if I was holding onto a pipe dream, but I'm thankful for so much more than just how God has kept me. God literally saved my life and put this dream on my heart. And so, without God, none of this matters.

Now, to the village that God put around me. I am so incredibly grateful to the countless people who helped me realize a dream that I've had since I was a second grade student creating her first book for class. I am especially thankful for my amazing agent, Latoya C. Smith. Without your belief in me and my vision, I wouldn't be here. You helped me take a very rough draft with a lot of promise and turn it into something that exceeded even my expectations. But you didn't stop there. You've pushed me, guided me with important decisions, had my back at every turn, and taken me under your wing in a way that I can't express fully in words. Perhaps most importantly, you led me to Harlequin and to Gail.

Gail Chasan, your enthusiasm for this book and for my work is contagious, even to me! You have been the celebratory rock in my corner from the moment Latoya connected us, and I couldn't be happier to be on the Latoya/Gail dream team with such fantastic thought partners and ship steerers. From the moment we first virtually met, you got the story I was trying to tell. That's every writer's dream come true. Megan Broderick, you've answered every single question I've had (and there were many) with such ease and have been the biggest help as I've navigated new and exciting things like art sheets and rounds of edits and book prelims. You have taken such good care of my book baby at every step, and I'm truly thankful. Each of y'all are legit my sheroes, as are the rest of the Harlequin family—from the art team (yess first book cover!) to copy editors to marketing to author communications and everyone in between, I've continued to be in awe of your support and excitement for this project. You make it easy to want to shout that I'm a Harlequin author!

My family is also out of this world. The support you all have given me can't be quantified, but whether it was messaging me from Japan just to ask how my writing was going, showing up to every virtual event I've participated in, or simply reminding me that I was called to do this over and over again, I've needed y'all more than I've said. And yet, somehow, I never had to say it. To Mom, Dad, Mawmaw, Brittany, Marley, Amber, Tayler, Glen, Lana, Jason, Aunt Leslie, Uncle Curt, and so so many others, thank you for believing in me and showing up for me always. You all are my innermost circle, and I'm thankful you've let me lean on you like I do.

To Enjoli, Cora, Nyanquoi, Candice, Erika, Katy, Anna, Maranda, Amanda, Ashleigh, Talia, Carla, Aria, Xayna, Anika, Lakelle, Lloyd, Ebony, Barbara, Aghogho, Selena, Tim, Amie, Keila, Keith, Michael A., Brittney C., Shaton, Amir, Kimberly, Canisha, Soraya, Erlie, Brenda, Michael L., Charreah, Alison B., Jackie, Jenna, Ruschelle, Renee, Nicole J., Floyd, and so many others, thank you for being my guide posts. Thank you for your various counsels over the years, for the times I brainstormed ideas with you, or maybe even told you that something that happened in your life inspired a piece of my book and you didn't recoil lol. Thank you for your constant encouragement, for talking me down from bouts of overthinking, stepping in to remind me of the promise God made to me long ago, and checking me when I was editing the same chapter over and again. You all have even been editors and thought partners before I had professional editors and thought partners—and still are! I'm not here without you.

Lastly, thank you to the other authors I've met in real life, or just in my head, who to this day continue to inspire me. Whether it was a chance meeting in Union Station in DC, or we spoke on a panel together (and you've been in my corner ever since), your storytelling and the way you approach life pushes me to be better, kinder, more vulnerable, more giving, and of course, a better writer. That kind of motivation is not something I could ever repay.

I've named a lot of people in these acknowledgments, and in truth, there's probably so many more I could have added to these lists. For there has never been a time that I can remember when I wasn't dreaming to be a published author and having the opportunity to tell the extraordinary stories of ordinary people around the world, but there's also no world in which this dream is just mine. I am the luckiest girl on planet Earth to be able to share it with all y'all.

The best is yet to come! (#Nkiruka)

#2893 ANYONE BUT A FORTUNE

The Fortunes of Texas: The Wedding Gift • by Judy Duarte

Self-made woman Sofia De Leon has heard enough about the old-money Fortune family to know that Beau Fortune is not to be trusted. And now that they are competing for the same business award, he is also her direct rival. It is just a hot Texas minute, though, before ambition begins warring with attraction...

#2894 FIRST COMES BABY...

Wild Rose Sisters • by Christine Rimmer

When Josie LeClaire went into labor alone on her farm, she had no one to turn to but her nearby fellow farmer, Miles Halstead. Fortunately, the widowed Miles was more than up to the task. But a marriage of convenience is only convenient until one side ends up with unrequited feelings. Will Miles be willing to let go of his fears, or will Josie be the one left out in the cold?

#2895 HOME IS WHERE THE HOUND IS

Furever Yours • by Melissa Senate

Animal rescue worker Bethany Robeson already has her hands full with an inherited house and an overweight pooch named Meatball. She doesn't dare make room for Shane Dupree, her former high school sweetheart, now a single dad. Bethany doesn't believe in starting over, but Shane, baby Wyatt and Meatball could be the family she always dreamed of...

#2896 THE WRANGLER RIDES AGAIN

Men of the West • by Stella Bagwell

For years, rugged cowboy Jim Carroway has been more at home with horses than with people. But when stunning nanny Tallulah O'Brien arrives to wrangle the kids of Three Rivers Ranch, she soon tempts him from the barn back to life. After Jim lost his pregnant wife, he thought he'd closed his heart forever. Can the vibrant, vivacious Tally convince him that it's never too late for love's second act?

#2897 THE HERO NEXT DOOR

Small-Town Sweethearts • by Carrie Nichols

Olive Downing has big dreams for her Victorian bed-and-breakfast. She doesn't need her handsome new neighbor pointing out the flaws in her plan. But Cal Pope isn't the average busybody. The gruff firefighter can be sweet, charming—and the perfect partner for the town fundraiser. Maybe there's a soft heart underneath his rough exterior that needs rescuing, too?

#2898 A MARRIAGE OF BENEFITS

Home to Oak Hollow • by Makenna Lee

Veterinarian Jessica Talbot wants to build a clinic and wildlife rescue. She could access her trust fund, but there's a caveat—Jessica needs a husband. When she learns Officer Jake Carter needs funding to buy and train his own K-9 partner, Jessica proposes. Jake is shocked, but he agrees—only for the money. It's the perfect plan—if only Jessica can avoid falling for her husband...and vice versa!

HSECNM0122B

Bethany Robeson already has her hands full with an inherited house and an overweight pooch named Meatball. She doesn't dare make room for Shane Dupree, her former high school sweetheart, now a single dad. Bethany doesn't believe in starting over, but Shane, baby Wyatt and Meatball could be the family she always dreamed of...

Read on for a sneak peek of the latest book in the Furever Yours continuity, Home is Where the Hound Is *by Melissa Senate!*

"I remember. I remember it all, Bethany."

Jeez. He hadn't meant for his voice to turn so serious, so reverent. But there was very little chance of hiding his real feelings when she was around.

"Me, too," she said.

For a few moments they ate in silence.

"Thanks for helping me here," she said. "You've done a lot of that since I've been back."

"Anytime. And I mean that."

"Ditto," she said.

He reached over and squeezed her hand but didn't let go. And suddenly he was looking—with that seriousness, with that reverence—into those green eyes that had also kept him up those nights when he couldn't stop thinking about her. They both leaned in at the same time, the kiss soft, tender, then with all the pent-up passion they'd clearly both been feeling these last days.

She pulled slightly away. "Uh-oh."

He let out a rough exhale, trying to pull himself together. "Right? You're leaving in a couple weeks. Maybe three tops. And I'm solely focused on being the best father I can be. So that's two really good reasons why we shouldn't kiss again." Except he leaned in again.

And so did she. This time there was nothing soft or tender about the kiss. Instead, it was pure passion. His hand wound in her silky brown hair, her hands on his face.

A puppy started barking, then another, then yet another. The three cockapoos.

"They're saving us from getting into trouble," Bethany said, glancing at the time on her phone. "Time for their potty break. They'll be interrupting us all night, so that should keep us in line."

He smiled. "We can get into a lot of trouble in between, though."

Don't miss
Home is Where the Hound Is *by Melissa Senate,
available March 2022 wherever
Harlequin Special Edition books and ebooks are sold.*

Harlequin.com

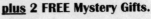

Love Harlequin romance?

DISCOVER.

Be the first to find out about promotions,
news and exclusive content!

Facebook.com/HarlequinBooks

Twitter.com/HarlequinBooks

Instagram.com/HarlequinBooks

Pinterest.com/HarlequinBooks

YouTube.com/HarlequinBooks

ReaderService.com

EXPLORE.

Sign up for the Harlequin e-newsletter and
download a free book from any series at
TryHarlequin.com

CONNECT.

Join our Harlequin community to
share your thoughts and connect
with other romance readers!
Facebook.com/groups/HarlequinConnection